WHAT ARE YOU LOOKING FOR?

Also by the same author in Aleph

*Can the Mind Be Quiet?: Living, Learning, and Meditation*

{366}

# WHAT ARE YOU LOOKING FOR?

JIDDU KRISHNAMURTI

ALEPH

ALEPH

ALEPH BOOK COMPANY
An independent publishing firm
promoted by ***Rupa Publications India***

Published in India in 2023
by Aleph Book Company
7/16 Ansari Road, Daryaganj
New Delhi 110 002


Krishnamurti Foundation of America
P.O. Box 1560, Ojai, California 93024
United States of America

E-mail: info@kfa.org. Website: www.kfa.org

For further information about J. Krishnamurti please visit: www.jkrishnamurti.org



ISBN: 978-93-95853-64-4

1 3 5 7 9 10 8 6 4 2



Printed in India.

# CONTENTS

SECTION THREE: WHAT IS THE PURPOSE OF LIFE?

# FOREWORD

Jiddu Krishnamurti (1895–1986) is regarded internationally as one of the great educators and philosophers of our time. Born in South India, he was educated in England, and traveled the world, giving public talks, holding dialogues, writing, and founding schools until the end of his life at the age of ninety. He claimed allegiance to no caste, nationality, or religion and was bound by no tradition.

*Time* magazine named Krishnamurti, along with Mother Teresa, "one of the five saints of the 20th century," and the Dalai Lama calls Krishnamurti "one of the greatest thinkers of the age."

His teachings are published in 75 books and over 4 million copies of his books have been sold in over 30 languages. The rejection of all spiritual and psychological authority, including his own, is a fundamental theme. He said human beings have to free themselves of fear, conditioning, authority, and dogma through self-knowledge. He suggested that this will bring about order and real psychological change. Our violent, conflict-ridden world cannot be transformed into a life of goodness, love, and compassion by any political, social, or economic strategies. It can be transformed only through mutation in individuals brought about through their own observation without any guru or organized religion.

Krishnamurti's stature as an original philosopher attracted traditional and also creative people from all walks of life. Heads of state, eminent scientists, prominent leaders of the United Nations and various religious organizations, psychiatrists and psychologists, and university professors all engaged in dialogue with Krishnamurti. Students, teachers, and millions of people from all walks of life read his books and came to hear him speak. He bridged science and religion without the use of jargon, so scientists and lay people alike could understand his discussions of time, thought, insight, and death.

During his lifetime, Krishnamurti established foundations in the United States, India, England, Canada, and Spain. Their defined role is the preservation and dissemination of the teachings, but without any authority to interpret or deify the teachings or the person.

Krishnamurti also founded schools in India, England, and the United States. He envisioned that education should emphasize the understanding of the whole human being, mind and heart, not the mere acquisition of academic and intellectual skills. Education must be for learning skills in the art of living, not only the technology to make a living.

Krishnamurti said, "Surely a school is a place where one learns about the totality, the wholeness of life. Academic excellence is absolutely necessary, but a school includes much more than that. It is a place where both the teacher and the taught explore, not only the outer world, the world of knowledge, but also their own thinking, their behavior."

He said of his work, "There is no belief demanded or asked, there are no followers, there are no cults, there is no persuasion of any kind, in any direction, and therefore only then we can meet on the same platform, on the same ground, at the same level. Then we can together observe the extraordinary phenomena of human existence."

R. E. Mark Lee,
Executive Director,
Krishnamurti Foundation of America.

# INTRODUCTION

We all live in relationship. We live in relationship to one another, to our families, to the world, to the earth, and the universe. Because all life is lived in relationship, it is essential that we understand what relationship is, and what every movement in relationship—to lovers, parents, friends, teachers, society—can mean to us and to everyone else.

Put together, all our individual relationships create society. Society is us. So what we are in relationship, each one of us, creates society. If we are angry, jealous, aggressively ambitious, self-pityingly lonely, depressed, prejudiced, exclusive in relationship, we create a society that is crazy. Multiply each self-centered or affectionate, greedy or generous one of us in relationship with another by 6 billion—and that is our world. Everything we are affects everything else: people, animals, earth, biosphere. As you can see, this goes both ways.

Every evil affects us all; but so does every good. Most of us realize, when we are not too scared to look at it, that we are very lonely people. We don't know why or how it happens, but even in our own families, even among our friends, and even with a boyfriend or girlfriend, we often feel isolated and lonely. Even in the most intimate relationship with somebody, we are thinking about ourselves, our fears of being abandoned, our insecurities. The result is even more loneliness, more dependency on people and things, and the suffering that comes from all that. We have made such a habit of all this fear and suffering, we forget, or have never been taught, that these habits, biological and cultural as well as personal habits, can be changed. It is true we have inherited aggressive survival and territorial instincts from our ancestors, the animals we once were; but our brains also have the intelligence to decide when those are appropriate and when to change our behavior.

It seems strange that we have not been taught about relationship—to oneself, to others, to work, money, society, to the earth and the universe—in school. Since our very survival, personally and collectively, depends on relationship, you might think educators and parents would insist we learn about relationship right along with reading, writing, math, and computers. We are taught to make a living, but not how to live. So we must each learn on our own the art of relationship, of living itself.

We must learn what relationship is, what it is not, what goes wrong. Though outwardly we may be clever and cultured, inwardly humans are still violent. True education is changing the inner human being. The key to right relationship is to understand our own thinking, which is self-knowledge—the ability to understand all the ways we have been conditioned to think and behave by our personal experience, our families, our culture, country, religions, our gender and biology.

If you don't understand your own thinking, whatever you do think has little meaning. Without knowledge of your own biases and the impediments of biological or personal prejudice, without understanding your fears, your hurt, your anger, without the ability to see through and beyond them, all your thinking, all your relationships will be fogged or skewed. After all, self-knowledge is the basis for relationship.

You can find the truth about yourself in the most available mirror of all—the mirror of relationship itself. You can see how you feel, what you think, how you behave just by carefully watching how you are in encounters with the people in your life every day. You can see in your reactions to others what makes you angry, what hurts you, when you are generous, joyful, fully alive. Remember not to write your findings in cement: life changes every minute, and so do you. Just notice what you are feeling. You don't need to act it out or stuff it to act on later. Not acting on anger or greed is very difficult. But even if it is difficult, it does not mean there is something wrong with you. It is just plain hard work rewiring the conditioning of millions of years of aggressive, hunter tribalism. But if you can learn from one angry moment, it is significant. Each time you can do it, there is one less drop of poison in the air we all breathe.

This kind of self-knowledge and alertness in behavior brings freedom to your life and relationships. No longer will the wild horses in you drag you to places you don't want to go. Self-knowledge is also the key to survival: all human brains are more alike than unalike, and to understand yourself is to understand everyone else as well.

Thousands of generations have produced this world with its self-centered, me and my family and my country first ideas, the poison of separative organizations. We have to change it, or go on suffering the same way. Life is enormous.

If all we do is dig a hole, however comfortable, and crawl into it, we're going to miss the whole extraordinary experience of living. If all we choose is to relate to each other in the same painful way, because we are afraid to be insecure, we're all dead. We must choose: either to go the old way and suffer the pain of separation and loneliness; or to stand up against the old self-centered ways and live in love, not just with one person in particular, but with all life.

These talks and writings come from a man who lived like all society's great outsiders: the rebel; the wandering poet; the religious philosopher; the breakthrough scientists and psychologists; the great traveling teachers of all millennia.

For sixty-five years, Krishnamurti spoke of psychological freedom to whomever would listen. He founded schools where young people can study all the usual subjects—and themselves as well. In the schools, as in all the talks and writings, he points out that it is not our wars, inner and outer, that will set us free, but the truth about ourselves.

There is no path, no authority, no guru to follow: you have the capacity in yourself to find out what you are, what you are doing with your life, with your relationships, and with your work. It is up to you to experiment with what is said in this book. Someone else's opinion about you and the way you live your life is no more nourishing than someone else eating your dinner.

All of the selections in this volume are taken from Krishnamurti's books, his reported and recorded dialogues, and his public talks. Try the experiment of reading this book, and further sources listed in the back, and see for yourself what inward changes begin to happen.

Dale Carlson,
Editor.

SECTION ONE

# PEOPLE: PERSON TO PERSON

CHAPTER ONE

# WHAT IS RELATIONSHIP?

## — 1 —
## *All Life Is Relationship*

All life is a movement in relationship. There is no living thing on earth which is not related to something or other. Even the hermit, a man who goes off to a lonely spot, is related to the past, is related to those who are around him. There is no escape from relationship. In that relationship, which is the mirror in which we can see ourselves, we can discover what we are, our reactions, our prejudices, our fears, depression, anxieties, loneliness, sorrow, pain, grief. We can also discover whether we love, or there is no such thing as love. So, we will examine this question of relationship because that is the basis of love.

## — 2 —
## *Relationship Is a Means of Self-Discovery*

Relationship is a mirror in which I can see myself. That mirror can either be distorted, or it can be 'as is', reflecting that which is. But most of us see in relationship, in that mirror, things we would rather see; we do not see what is. We would rather idealize...

Now if we examine our life, our relationship with another, we shall see that it is a process of isolation. We are really not concerned with another; though we talk a great deal about it, actually we are not concerned. We are related to someone only so long as that relationship gratifies us, so long as it gives us a refuge, so long as it satisfies us. But the moment there is a disturbance in the relationship which produces discomfort in ourselves, we discard that relationship. In other words, there is relationship only so long as we are gratified. This may sound harsh, but if you really examine your life very closely you will see it is a fact...

If we look into our lives and observe relationship, we see it is a process of building resistance against another, a wall over which we look and observe the other; but we always retain the wall and remain behind it, whether it be a psychological wall, a material wall, an economic wall or a national wall. So long as we live in isolation, behind a wall, there is no relationship with another....The world is so disruptive, there is so much sorrow, so much pain, war, destruction, misery, that we want to escape and live within the walls of security, of our own psychological being. So, relationship with most of us is actually a process of isolation, and obviously such relationship builds a society that is also isolating. That is exactly what is happening throughout the world: you remain in your isolation and stretch your hand over the wall....

## — 3 —
## *Real Relationship or Only Images?*

What do we mean by that word? Are we ever related to anyone, or is the relationship between two images which we have created about each other? I have an image about you, and you have an image about me. I have an image about you as my wife or husband, or whatever it is, and you an image about me also. The relationship is between these two images and nothing else. To have relationship with another is only possible when there is no image.

When I can look at you and you can look at me without the image of memory, of insults, and all the rest, then there is a relationship, but the very nature of the observer is the image, isn't it? My image observes your image, if it is possible to observe it, and this is called relationship, but it is between two images, a relationship which is nonexistent because both are images. To be related means to be in contact. Contact must be something direct, not between two images. It requires a great deal of attention, an awareness, to look at another without the image that I have about that person, the image being my memories of that person—how he has insulted me, pleased me, given me pleasure, this or that. Only when there are no images between the two is there a relationship.

## — 4 —
## *Relationship Is a Mirror of Myself*

Surely, only in relationship the process of what I am unfolds, does it not? Relationship is a mirror in which I see myself as I am; but as most of us do not like what we are, we begin to discipline, either positively or negatively, what we perceive in the mirror of relationship. That is, I discover something in relationship, in the action of relationship, and I do not like it. So, I begin to modify what I do not like, what I perceive as being unpleasant. I want to change it—which means I already have a pattern of what I should be. The moment there is a pattern of what I should be, there is no comprehension of what I am. The moment I have a picture of what I want to be, or what I should be, or what I ought not to be—a standard according to which I want to change myself—then, surely, there is no comprehension of what I am at the moment of relationship.

I think it is really important to understand this, for I think this is where most of us go astray. We do not want to know what we actually are at a given moment in relationship. If we are concerned merely with self-improvement, there is no comprehension of ourselves, of.

## — 5 —
## *Self-Knowledge Is the Basis for Relationship: The Problem in Relationship Is Ourselves*

So, as our problems are the result of the total process of ourselves, which is action in relationship, whether with things, ideas, or people, it is essential, is it not, that there should be understanding of ourselves. Without knowing myself, I have no real basis for thinking.

## — 6 —
## *Security, Dependency, or Relationship*

Relationship is inevitably painful, which is shown in our everyday existence. If in relationship there is no tension, it ceases to be relationship and merely becomes a comfortable sleep-state, an opiate—which most people want and prefer.

Conflict is between this craving for comfort and the factual, between illusion and actuality. If you recognize the illusion then you can, by putting it aside, give your attention to the understanding of relationship. But if you seek security in relationship, it becomes an investment in comfort, in illusion—and the greatness of relationship is its very insecurity. By seeking security in relationship you are hindering its function, which brings its own peculiar actions and misfortunes.

Surely, the function of relationship is to reveal the state of one's whole being. Relationship is a process of self-revelation, of self-knowledge. This self-revelation is painful, demanding constant adjustment, pliability of thought-emotion.

It is a painful struggle, with periods of enlightened peace... But most of us avoid or put aside the tension in relationship, preferring the ease and comfort of satisfying dependency, an unchallenged security, a safe anchorage. Then family and other relationships become a refuge, the refuge of the thoughtless.

When insecurity creeps into dependency, as it inevitably does, then that particular relationship is cast aside and a new one is taken on in the hope of finding lasting security; but there is no security in relationship, and dependency only breeds fear. Without understanding the process of security and fear, relationship becomes a binding hindrance, a way of ignorance. Then all existence is struggle and pain, and there is no way out of it save in right thinking, which comes through self-knowledge.

## — 7 —
## *The Way You and I Relate to Each Other Creates Society*

We know what our relationship is at present—a contention, a struggle, a pain, or mere habit. If we can understand fully, completely, relationship with the one, then perhaps there is a possibility of understanding relationship with the many, that is, with society. If I do not understand my relationship with the one, I certainly shall not understand my relationship with the whole, with society, with the many. And if my relationship with the one is based on a need, on gratification, then my relationship with society must be the same....Is it possible to live, with the one and with the many, without demand? Surely, that is the problem—is it not?....As long as we use relationship as a means of gratification, of escape, as a distraction that is mere activity, there can be no self-knowledge.

But self-knowledge is understood, is uncovered, its process is revealed, through relationship; that is, if you are willing to go into the question of relationship and expose yourself to it. Because, after all, you cannot live without relationship. But we want to use that relationship to be comfortable, to be gratified, to be something.

## — 8 —
## *Relationship Is Not Just a Demand for Security Good Feelings, and Gratification*

So you see that relationship, if we allow it, can be a process of self-revelation, but since we do not allow it, relationship becomes merely a gratifying activity. As long as the mind merely uses relationship for its own security, that relationship is bound to create confusion and antagonism. Is it possible to live in relationship without the idea of demand, of want, of gratification?

— 9 —

### *When Relationship Is Only Idea, Thought, There is Conflict, Not Love*

You cannot think about love. You can think about the person whom you love, but thought is not love, and so, gradually, thought takes the place of love....Can relationship be based on an idea? If it is, is it not a self-enclosing activity, and therefore isn't it inevitable that there should be contention, strife, and misery?

— 10 —

### *Love Is not Gratification*

There can be true relationship only when there is love, but love is not the search for gratification. Love exists only when there is self-forgetfulness, when there is complete communion, not between one or two, but communion with the highest; and that can only take place when the self is forgotten.

— 11 —

### *Relationship and Dependence*

Now for most of us relationship with another is based on dependence, economic or psychological. This dependence creates fear, breeds in us possessiveness, results in friction, suspicion, frustration. Economic dependence on another can perhaps be eliminated through legislation and proper organization, but I am referring especially to that psychological dependence on another which is the outcome of craving for personal satisfaction, happiness, and so on. One feels, in this possessive relationship, enriched, creative, and active; one feels one's own little flame of being is increased by another and so in order not to lose this source of completeness one fears the loss of the other, and so possessive fears come into being with all their resulting problems. Thus in this relationship of psychological dependence, there must always be conscious or unconscious fear, suspicion, which often lies hidden in pleasant-sounding words... Though one is dependent on another, there is yet the desire to be inviolate, to be whole. The complex problem in relationship is how to love without dependence, without friction and conflict; how to conquer the desire to isolate oneself, to withdraw from the cause of conflict. If we depend for our happiness on another, on society, or on environment, they become essential to us; we cling to them and any alteration of these we violently oppose because we depend upon them for our psychological security and comfort. Though, intellectually, we may perceive that life is a continual process of flux, mutation, necessitating constant change, yet emotionally or sentimentally we cling to the established and comforting values; hence there is a constant battle between change and the desire for permanency. Is it possible to put an end to this conflict?

Life cannot be without relationship. But we have made it so agonizing and hideous by basing it on personal and possessive love. Can one love and yet not possess? You will find the true answer not in escape, ideals, beliefs, but through the understanding of the causes of dependence and possessiveness. If one can deeply understand this problem of relationship between oneself and another, then perhaps we shall understand and solve the problems of our relationship with society, for society is but the extension of ourselves.

The environment which we call society is created by past generations: we accept it, as it helps us to maintain our greed, possessiveness, illusion. In this illusion there cannot be unity or peace. Mere economic unity brought about through compulsion and legislation cannot end war. As long as we do not understand individual relationship, we cannot have a peaceful society. Since our relationship is based on possessive love, we have to become aware, in ourselves, of its birth, its causes, its action. In becoming deeply aware of the process of possessiveness with its violence, fears, its reactions, there comes an understanding that is whole, complete. This understanding alone frees thought from dependence and possessiveness. It is within oneself that harmony in relationship can be found, not in another, nor in environment.

In relationship, the primary cause of friction is oneself, the self that is the center of unified craving. If we can but realize that it is not how another acts that is of primary importance, but how each one of us acts and reacts, and if that reaction and action can be fundamentally, deeply understood, then relationship will undergo a deep and radical change. In this relationship with another, there is not only the physical problem but also that of thought and feeling on all levels, and one can be harmonious with another only when one is harmonious integrally in oneself. In relationship the important thing to bear in mind is not the other but oneself, which does not mean that one must isolate oneself but understand deeply in oneself the cause of conflict and sorrow. So long as we depend on another for our psychological well-being, intellectually or emotionally, that dependence must inevitably create fear from which arises sorrow.

## — 12 —
## *Where There Is Attachment, There Is No Love*

And is not our relationship with each other a state of psychological dependency? I am not talking about physiological interdependence, which is entirely different. I depend on my son because I want him to be something that I am not. He is the fulfillment of all my hopes, my desires; he is my immortality, my continuation. So my relationship with my son, with my wife, with my children, with my neighbors, is a state of psychological dependency, and I am fearful of being in a state in which there is no dependence. I do not know what that means, therefore I depend on books, on relationship, on society, I depend on property to give me security, position, prestige. And if I do not depend on any of these things, then I depend on the experiences that I have had, on my own thoughts, on the greatness of my own pursuits.

Psychologically, then, our relationships are based on dependence, and that is why there is fear. The problem is not how not to depend, but just to see the fact that we do depend.

Where there is attachment there is no love. Because you do not know how to love, you depend, and...where there is dependency there is fear. I am talking of psychological dependency, not of your dependence on the milkman to bring you milk, or your dependence on the railway, or on a bridge. It is this inward psychological dependency—on ideas, on people, on property that breeds fear. So, you cannot be free from fear as long as you do not understand relationship, and relationship can be understood only when the mind watches all its relationships, which is the beginning of self-knowledge.

Now, can you listen to all this easily, without effort? Effort exists only when you are trying to get something, when you are trying to be something. But if, without trying to be free from fear, you are able to listen to the fact that attachment destroys love, then that very fact will immediately free the mind from fear. There can be no freedom from fear as long as there is no understanding of relationship, which means, really, as long as there is no self-knowledge. The self is revealed only in relationship. In observing the way I talk to my neighbor, the way I regard property, the way I cling to belief or to experience or to knowledge; that is, in discovering my own dependency, I begin to awaken to the whole process of self-knowledge.

So, how to overcome fear is not important. You can take a drink and forget it. You can go to the temple and lose yourself in prostration, in muttering words, or in devotion, but fear waits around the corner when you come out. There is the cessation only when you understand your relationship to all things, and that understanding does not come into being if there is no self-knowledge. Self-knowledge is not something far away; it begins here, now, in observing how you treat your servants, your wife, your children. Relationship is the mirror in which you see yourself as you are. If you are capable of looking at yourself as you are without any evaluation, then there is the cessation of fear, and out of that comes an extraordinary sense of love. Love is something that cannot be cultivated; love is not a thing to be bought by the mind. If you say, "I am going to practice being compassionate," then compassion is a thing of the mind, and therefore not love.

Love comes into being darkly, unknowingly, fully, when we understand this whole process of relationship. Then the mind is quiet, it does not fill the heart with the things of the mind, and therefore that which is love can come into being.

## CHAPTER TWO

# LOVE, SEX, AND RELATIONSHIP

### — 1 —
### *We Have Two Problems*

So we have two problems—love and sex. The one is an abstract idea, the other is an actual daily biological urge—a fact that exists and cannot be denied. Let us first find out what love is, not as an abstract idea, but what it actually is. What is it? Is it merely a sensuous delight, cultivated by thought as pleasure, the remembrance of an experience which has given great delight or sexual enjoyment?....Does it exist without the object? Or does it come into being only because of the object?....Or is love a state in you...?

### — 2 —
### *What Is Love?*

What is love? Can we understand it verbally and intellectually, or is it something that cannot be put into words? What is it that each one of us calls love? Is love sentiment? Is love emotion? Can love be divided as divine and human? Is there love when there is jealousy or hatred or competitive drive? Is there love when each one of us is seeking his own security, both psychological as well as worldly, outwardly? Don't agree or disagree, because you are caught in this. We are not talking of some love that is abstract; an abstract idea of love has no value at all. You and I can have a lot of theories about it, but actually, what is the thing that we call love?

There is pleasure, sexual pleasure, in which there is jealousy, the possessive factor, the dominating factor, the desire to possess, to hold, to control, to interfere with what another thinks. Knowing all the complexity of this, we say that there must be love that is divine, that is beautiful, untouched, uncorrupted; we meditate about it and get into a devotional, sentimental, emotional attitude, and are lost. Because we can't fathom this human thing called love we run away into abstractions that have absolutely no validity at all. Right? So what is love? Is it pleasure and desire? Is it love of the one and not of the many?

To understand this question—what is love?—one must go into the problem of pleasure, sexual pleasure, or the pleasure of dominating another, of controlling or suppressing another; and whether love is of the one, denying the love of the other.

If one says, "I love you," does it exclude the other? Is love personal or impersonal? We think that if one loves one person, one can't love the whole, and if one loves mankind then one can't possibly love the particular. This all indicates, does it not, that we have ideas about what love should be? This is again the pattern, the code developed by the culture in which we live, or the pattern that one has cultivated for oneself. So for us, ideas about love matter much more than the fact; we have ideas of what love is, what it should be, what it is not. The religious saints, unfortunately for mankind, have established that to love a woman is something totally wrong; you cannot possibly come near their idea of God if you love someone.

That is, sex is taboo; it is pushed aside by the saints, but they are eaten up with it, generally. So to go into this question of what love is, one must first put away all ideas, all ideologies of what it is, or should be, or should not be, and the division as the divine and the not divine. Can we do that?

## — 3 —
## *What Love Is Not*

*Questioner*: What do you mean by love?

*Krishnamurti*: We are going to discover by understanding what love is not, because, as love is the unknown, we must come to it by discarding the known. The unknown cannot be discovered by a mind that is full of the known... What is love with most of us? When we say we love somebody, what do we mean? We mean we possess that person. From that possession arises jealousy, because if I lose him or her what happens? I feel empty, lost; therefore I legalize possession; I hold him or her. From holding, possessing that person, there is jealousy, there is fear, and all the innumerable conflicts that arise from possession. Surely such possession is not love, is it?

Obviously love is not sentiment. To be sentimental, to be emotional, is not love, because sentimentality and emotion are mere sensations. A religious person who weeps about Jesus or Krishna, about their guru or somebody else, is merely sentimental, emotional. They are indulging in sensation, which is a process of thought, and thought is not love. Thought is the result of sensation, so the person who is sentimental, who is emotional, cannot possibly know love. Again, aren't we emotional and sentimental? Sentimentality, emotionalism, is merely a form of self-expansion. To be full of emotion is obviously not love, because a sentimental person can be cruel when their sentiments are not responded to, when their feelings have no outlet. An emotional person can be stirred to hatred, to war, to butchery. Someone who is sentimental, full of tears for their religion, surely has no love.

Is forgiveness love? What is implied in forgiveness? You insult me and I resent it, remember it; then, either through compulsion or through repentance, I say, "I forgive you." First I retain and then I reject. Which means what? I am still the central figure. I am still important, it is I who am forgiving somebody. As long as there is the attitude of forgiving it is I who am important, not the man who is supposed to have insulted me. So when I accumulate resentment and then deny that resentment, which you call forgiveness, it is not love. A man who loves obviously has no enmity and to all these things he is indifferent. Sympathy, forgiveness, the relationship of possessiveness, jealousy, and fear—all these things are not love. They are all of the mind, are they not?... The mind can only corrupt love, it cannot give birth to love, it cannot give beauty. You can write a poem about love, but that is not love.

Obviously there is no love when there is no real respect, when you don't respect another, whether he is your servant or your friend. Have you not noticed that you are not respectful, kindly, generous, to your servants, to people who are so called "below" you? You have respect for those above, for your boss, for the millionaire, for the man with a large house and a title, for the man who can give you a better position, a better job, from whom you can get something. But you kick those below you...

You can know love only when all these things have stopped, come to an end....How few of us are generous, forgiving, merciful! You are generous when it pays you, you are merciful when you can see something in return. When these things disappear, when these things don't occupy your mind and when the things of the mind don't fill your heart, then there is love; and love alone can transform the present madness and insanity in the world—not systems, not theories...

The practice of love, the practice of brotherhood, is still within the field of the mind, therefore it is not love. When all this has stopped, then love comes into being, then you will know what it is to love. Then love is not quantitative but qualitative. You do not say, "I love the whole world," but when you know how to love one, you know how to love the whole. Because we do not know how to love one, our love of humanity is fictitious. When you love, there is neither one nor many: there is only love. It is only when there is love that all our problems can be solved....

## — 4 —
## *Why Have We Made Sex a Problem?*

*Questioner*: We know sex as an inescapable physical and psychological necessity and it seems to be a root cause of chaos in the personal life of our generation. How can we deal with this problem?

*Krishnamurti*: Why is it that whatever we touch we turn into a problem? We have made God a problem, we have made love a problem, we have made relationship, living a problem, and we have made sex a problem. Why? Why is everything we do a problem, a horror? Why are we suffering? Why has sex become a problem? Why do we submit to living with problems, why do we not put an end to them? Why do we not die to our problems instead of carrying them day after day, year after year? Sex is certainly a relevant question but there is the primary question: why do we make life into a problem? Working, sex, earning money, thinking, feeling, experiencing—you know, the whole business of living—why is it a problem? Is it not essentially because we always think from a particular point of view, from a fixed point of view? What do we mean by the problem of sex? Is it the act, or is it a thought about the act? Surely it is not the act. The sexual act is no problem to you, any more than eating is a problem to you, but if you think about eating or anything else all day long because you have nothing else to think about, it becomes a problem to you. Is the sexual act the problem or is it the thought about the act? Why do you think about it? Why do you build it up, which you are obviously doing? The cinemas, the magazines, the stories, everything is building up your thought of sex. Why does the mind build it up, why does the mind think about sex at all? Why? Why has it become a central issue in your life? When there are so many things calling, demanding your attention, you give complete attention to the thought of sex. What happens, why are your minds so occupied with it? Because that is a way of ultimate escape, is it not? It is a way of complete self-forgetfulness. For the time being, at least for that moment, you can forget yourself—and there is no other way of forgetting yourself. Everything else you do in life gives emphasis to the 'me', to the self. Your business, your religion, your gods, your leaders, your political and economic actions, your escapes, your social activities, your joining one party and rejecting another—all that is emphasizing and giving strength to the 'me'. That is, there is only one act in which there is no emphasis on the 'me', so it becomes a problem, does it not? When there is only one thing in your life that is an avenue to ultimate escape, to complete forgetfulness of yourself if only for a few seconds, you cling to it because that is the only moment in which you are happy. Every other issue you touch becomes a nightmare, a source of suffering and pain, so you cling to the one thing which gives complete self-forgetfulness, which you call happiness. But when you cling to it, it too becomes a nightmare, because then you want to be free from it, you do not want to be a slave to it. So you invent, again from the mind, the idea of chastity, of celibacy, and you try to be celibate, to be chaste, through suppression, all of which are operations of the mind to cut itself off from the fact. This again gives particular emphasis to the 'me' who is trying to become something, so again you are caught in travail, in trouble, in effort, in pain.

Sex becomes an extraordinarily difficult and complex problem so long as you do not understand the mind that thinks about the problem. The act itself can never be a problem but the thought about the act creates the problem.

## — 5 —
## *What Is Desire?*

Desire is energy, and it has to be understood; it cannot merely be suppressed, or made to conform...If you destroy desire, you destroy sensitivity, as well as the intensity that is necessary for the understanding of truth.

## — 6 —
## *Desire Is Not Love*

Desire is not love: desire leads to pleasure; desire is pleasure. We are not denying desire. It would be utterly stupid to say that we must live without desire, for that is impossible.

Man has tried that. People have denied themselves, tortured themselves, and yet desire has persisted, creating conflict, and all the brutalizing effects of that conflict. We are not advocating desirelessness, but we must understand the whole phenomena of desire, pleasure, and pain, and if we can go beyond there is a bliss and ecstasy, which is love.

## — 7 —
## *There Is Nothing Wrong with Desire*

Now what is desire? When I see a tree swaying in the wind, it is a lovely thing to watch, and what is wrong with that? What is wrong in watching the beautiful motion of a bird on the wing? What is wrong in looking at a new car, marvelously built and highly polished? And what is wrong in seeing a nice person with a symmetrical face, a face that shows good sense, intelligence, quality?

## — 8 —
## *The Problem Is Not Desire, but the Afterthought, 'I Must Have That'*

But desire does not stop there. Your perception is not just perception, but with it comes sensation. With the arising of sensation you want to touch, to contact, and then comes the urge to possess. You say, "This is beautiful, I must have it," and so begins the turmoil of desire.

Now, is it possible to see, to observe, to be aware of the beautiful and the ugly things of life, and not say, "I must have," or "I must not have"? Have you ever just observed anything? Do you understand? Have you ever observed your wife, your children, your friends, just looked at them? Have you ever looked at a flower without calling it a rose, without wanting to put it in your button-hole, or take it home and give it to somebody? If you are capable of so observing, without all the values attributed by the mind, then you will find that desire is not such a monstrous thing. You can look at a car, see the beauty of it, and not be caught in the turmoil or contradiction of desire. But that requires an immense intensity of observation, not just a casual glance. It is not that you have no desire, but simply that the mind is capable of looking without describing. It can look at the moon and not immediately say, "That is the moon, how beautiful it is," so there is no chattering of the mind coming in between. If you can do this, you will find that in the intensity of observation, of feeling, of real affection, love has its own action, which is not the contradictory action of desire.

## — 9 —
## *Can We Love without the Desire to Possess?*

Experiment with this and you will see how difficult it is for the mind to observe without chattering about what it observes.

But surely, love is of that nature, is it not? How can you love if your mind is never silent, if you are always thinking about yourself? To love a person with your whole being, with your mind, heart, and body, requires great intensity; and when love is intense, desire soon disappears. But most of us have never had this intensity about anything, except about our own profit, conscious or unconscious; we never feel for anything without seeking something else out of it.

## — 10 —
## *Desire Is the Beginning of Love*

So, the understanding of desire is necessary. You have "to understand desire," not "to be without desire." If you kill desire, you are paralyzed. When you look at that sunset in front of you, the very looking is a delight, if you are at all sensitive. That is also desire—the delight. And if you cannot see that sunset and delight in it, you are not sensitive. If you cannot see a rich man in a big car and delight in that—not because you want it but you are just delighted to see a man in a big car—or if you cannot see a poor, unwashed, dirty, uneducated human being in despair and feel enormous pity, affection, love, you are not sensitive. How can you then find reality if you have not this sensitivity and feeling? So you have to understand desire... Then out of that understanding comes love. Most of us do not have love, we do not know what it means. We know pleasure, we know pain. We know the inconsistency of pleasure and, probably, the continuous pain. And we know the pleasure of sex and the pleasure of achieving fame, position, prestige.... We are everlastingly talking about love, but we do not know what it means, because we have not understood desire, which is the beginning of love....

## — 11 —
## *How Does Passion Come?*

So, someone who would understand desire, has to understand, has to listen to every prompting of the mind and the heart, to every mood, to every change of thought and feeling, has to watch it; they have to become sensitive, become alive to it. You cannot become alive to desire if you condemn it or compare it. You must care for desire, because it will give you an enormous understanding. And out of that understanding there is sensitivity. You are then sensitive, not only physically to beauty, to the dirt, to the stars, to a smiling face or to tears, but also to all the mutterings, the whispers that are in your minds, the secret hopes and fears. And out of this listening, watching, comes passion, this passion which is akin to love.

## — 12 —
## *Trouble Comes when Thought Works on Desire*

There is something pleasurable when I feel desire, and I give it continuity by thinking about it. One thinks about sex. You think about it and you give it a continuity. Or you think about the pain you had yesterday, the misery; and so you give that also continuity. So the rising of desire is natural, inevitable; you must have desire, you must react; otherwise you are a dead entity. But what is important is to see, to find out for yourself, when to give continuity to it and when not to.

So you have to understand then the structure of thought, which influences and controls and shapes and gives continuity to desire. Right? That is clear. Thought functions according to memory and so on—into which we are not going right now. We are just indicating how desire is strengthened by thinking about it constantly and giving it a continuity—which becomes the will. And with that will we operate. And that will is based on pleasure and on pain. If it is pleasurable, I want more of it; if it is painful, I resist it. So the resistance to pain or the pursuit of pleasure—both give continuity to desire...the moment you indulge in desire, it brings its own pain, its own pleasure, and you are back again in the vicious circle.

## — 13 —
## *It Is Thought that Turns Sex into Lust*

Thought, as we have said, sustains pleasure in thinking about something that has been pleasurable, cultivating the image, the picture. Thought engenders pleasure. Thinking about the sexual act becomes lust, which is entirely different from the act of sex. What most people are concerned with is the passion of lust. Craving before and after sex is lust. This craving is thought. Thought is not love.

*Questioner*: Can there be sex without this desire of thought?

*Krishnamurti*: You have to find out for yourself. Sex plays an extraordinarily important part in our lives because it is perhaps the only deep, first-hand experience we have. Intellectually and emotionally we conform, imitate, follow, obey.

There is pain and strife in all our relationships, except in the act of sex. This act being so different and beautiful, we become addicted to, so it in turn becomes a bondage. The bondage is the demand for its continuation—again the action of the center which is divisive. One is so hedged about—intellectually, in the family, in the community. Through social morality, through religious sanctions—so hedged about that there is only this one relationship left in which there is freedom and intensity. Therefore we give tremendous importance to it.

But if there were freedom all around then this would not be such a craving and such a problem. We make it a problem because we can't get enough of it, or because we feel guilty at having got it, or because in getting it we break the rules which society has laid down. It is the old society which calls the new society permissive because for the new society sex is a part of life. In freeing the mind from the bondage of imitation, authority, conformity, and religious prescriptions, sex has its own place, but it won't be all-consuming. From this one can see that freedom is essential for love—not the freedom of revolt, not the freedom of doing what one likes nor of indulging openly or secretly one's cravings, but rather the freedom which lies in the understanding of this whole structure and nature of the center. Then freedom is love.

*Questioner*: So freedom is not license?

*Krishnamurti*: No. License is bondage. Love is not hate, nor jealousy, nor ambition, nor the competitive spirit with its fear of failure. It is not the love of God nor the love of man—which again is a division. Love is not of the one or of the many. When there is love it is personal and impersonal, with and without an object. It is like the perfume of a flower; one or many can smell it: what matters is the perfume, not to whom it belongs.

## — 14 —
## *The Problem Is Not Sex but Lack of Love*

When we are young, we have strong sexual urges, and most of us try to deal with these desires by controlling and disciplining them, because we think that without some kind of restraint we shall become consumingly lustful. Organized religions are much concerned about our sexual morality; but they allow us to perpetrate violence and murder in the name of patriotism, to indulge in envy and crafty ruthlessness, and to pursue power and success. Why should they be so concerned with this particular type of morality, and not attack exploitation, greed, and war? Is it not because organized religions, being part of the environment which we have created, depend for their very existence on our fears and hopes, on our envy and separatism? So, in the religious field as in every other, the mind is held in the projections of its own desires.

As long as there is no deep understanding of the whole process of desire, the institution of marriage as it now exists, whether in the East or in the West, cannot provide the answer to the sexual problem. Love is not induced by the signing of a contract, nor is it based on an exchange of gratification, nor on mutual security and comfort. All these things are of the mind, and that is why love occupies so small a place in our lives. Love is not of the mind; it is wholly independent of thought with its cunning calculations, its self-protective demands and reactions. When there is love, sex is never a problem—it is the lack of love that creates the problem.

## — 15 —
## *Why Do We Think about Sex?*

Why does the mind think about sex at all? Why? Why has it become a central issue in your life? Sex becomes an extraordinary, difficult and complex problem so long as you do not understand the mind which thinks about the problem. The act itself can never be a problem but the thought about the act creates the problem.

CHAPTER THREE

# BOYFRIENDS AND GIRLFRIENDS

## — 1 —

## *Why Does Relationship Become Dependence?*

Physically we depend on the postman, on the milkman, on the supermarket. When we talk about dependence, what do we mean by that word? Is all relationship dependent?... Analytically one can discover clearly why one depends. One is empty, insufficient within oneself; one does not have sufficient energy, drive, capacity, clarity; one depends upon another to satisfy that insufficiency, that lack of perception, the sense of not being able to stand by oneself morally, intellectually, emotionally, physically. One also depends because one wants to be secure. The first thing a child demands is security. Most people want security, in which is implied comfort.

All these things are involved when one tries to find out why one depends emotionally, intellectually, and spiritually. I depend on you because you give me pleasure, you give me comfort, you give me satisfaction, you give me a sense of security, a balance, a harmony, a companionship, a togetherness.

We are going to examine presently whether it's real or unreal. I cling to you emotionally, physically, intellectually, or in some other way. In myself I'm isolated; I feel separate from everyone else. That separation is very painful. The demand to identify with another springs from that sense of isolation.

Please don't accept what I am saying; we are examining, analyzing, going into it together.

## — 2 —
## *Why Do I Want a Boyfriend or a Girlfriend So Much?*

Being isolated, we try to reach out for a companion, for friendship, for something that we can cling to. This is going on all around us, intellectually, emotionally, physically, in the deeper levels of consciousness—a constant demand to find someone, some idea, some hope, some kind of thing that will give a tremendous sense of being, a sense of identification with another or with ourselves. We do it because there is a sense of emptiness, of loneliness, of insufficiency in the ever self-centered activities...Having hooked on to someone or to some idea, in that very process there is an uncertainty, there is a fear that the thing we are attached to may be rather pliable, insecure. We become jealous, aggressive, demanding, possessive, dominating, and the battle begins.

You want to be free, and I can't let you be free. You want to look at someone else, and instantly I'm confused, lost, jealous, anxious. This process is called relationship. To be in contact with another is relationship, but I'm not in contact with anyone because out of my fear, out of my loneliness, out of my anxiety, out of all my self-centered activities, I hold on. How can I be sure of another?...I can't be sure of anything, but I want to be completely grounded in my security with another...

You can't let go. What is important is not letting go but finding out why you are dependent. If that is clear, then it's finished. Otherwise you may let one person go, but you will cling to someone else.

## — 3 —
## *We Call It Love*

We call it love; we call it protection; we give dozens of absurd words to it, but we have never really inquired into what relationship is. We are related because of inner uncertainty, the demand for security, the demand to be assured that we are related. It is a deeper, more subtle dependence than the physical. If we did not depend, what would happen? We'd be lost; we'd have no anchorage; there would be no port where we could say, "Here I'm at home...."

## — 4 —
## *Passion or Lust, the Beauty in Sex*

Wherever thought builds up the image of pleasure it must inevitably be lust and not the freedom of passion. If pleasure is the main drive then it is lust. When sexual feeling is born out of pleasure it is lust. If it is born out of love it is not lust, even though great delight may then be present....The beauty in sex is the absence of the 'me', the ego, but the thought of sex is the affirmation of this ego, and that is pleasure....

*Questioner*: What is passion itself, then?

*Krishnamurti*: It is to do with joy and ecstasy, which is not pleasure. In pleasure there is always a subtle form of effort—a seeking, craving, demanding, struggling to keep it, to get it.

In passion there is no demand and therefore no struggle. In passion there is not the slightest passion of fulfillment, therefore there can be neither frustration nor pain. Passion is the freedom from the 'me'...therefore passion is the essence of life. It is this that moves and lives. But when thought brings in all the problems of having and holding, then passion ceases.

## — 5 —
## *Why Has Sex Become So Important?*

How is it possible to meet the sexual demand intelligently and not turn it into a problem?

Now, what do we mean by sex? The purely physical act, or the thought that excites, stimulates, furthers that act?...

Why is it that sex has become such a problem in our lives?...

Sex is a problem because it would seem that in the act there is complete absence of the self. In that moment you are happy because there is the cessation of self-consciousness, of the 'me', and desiring more of it—more of the abnegation of the self in which there is complete happiness through full fusion, integration—naturally it becomes all-important. Isn't that so? Because it is something that gives me unadulterated joy, complete self-forgetfulness, I want more and more of it.

Now, why do I want more of it? Because, everywhere else I am in conflict....In all our relationships with property, with people, with ideas there is conflict, pain, struggle, misery...

Naturally you want more of it because it gives you happiness, while all the rest leads you to misery...

So, the problem is not sex, surely, but how to be free from the self. You have tasted that state of being in which the self is not, if only for a few seconds, if only for a day...so there is the constant longing for more of that self-free state...

Until you resolve the whole content of that conflict, this one release of the self, through sex, will remain a hideous problem...

## — 6 —
## *Love Is Not Just Sex*

And how can you have love? Surely, love is not a thing of the mind, is it? Love is not merely the sexual act, is it? Love is something which the mind can not possibly conceive...

There is love only when there is complete self-forgetfulness, and to have that blessing of love, one must be free through understanding relationship. Then, when there is love, the sexual act has quite a different significance. Then that act is not an escape, is not habit...love is a state of being.

## — 7 —
## *Homosexuality Is a Fact Like Heterosexuality*

There are people who have considerable difficulty with the fact of homosexuality. Teachers, for centuries, have avoided this question....This has been a question for thousands and thousands of years....As heterosexuality is a fact, homosexuality exists in the world. Why do we make it into such an enormous problem? Apparently we don't make heterosexuality a problem at all, but we make this into a problem, why? It is a fact. So should we inquire into this question, into heterosexuality, and homosexuality differently? Not condemn one or the other, or approve one and deny the other, but inquire why sexuality, both, has become so colossally important.

## — 8 —
## *We Don't Try to Change a Mountain or a Bird, so Why Sexual Preference?*

It is only the free mind, free brain that has no problems, that can meet problems and resolve them immediately.... We have problems in relationship between man and woman, or between man and man—homosexuality, in this country, more and more, not that it doesn't exist in other countries, but here it is becoming—you know all about it. Look at it very closely, observe it, not try to change it, try to direct it, say, "it must not be this way," or "it must be that way," or "help me to get over it," but just to observe. You can't change the line of that mountain, or the flight of the bird, or the flow of the water, swift, you just observe it and see the beauty of it.

But if you observe and say, "that is not so beautiful as the mountain I saw yesterday," you are not observing, you are merely comparing.

## — 9 —
## *Significance of Sharing, Being in Communion with Another*

Life is a constant movement in relationship. And if one is at all alert, awake to all the events that are going on in the world, this movement which is life must be understood, not at any particular level—scientific, biological, or traditional, or at the level of acquiring knowledge—but at the total level.

Otherwise, one cannot share.

You know that word has an extraordinary significance.

We may share money, clothes. If we have a little food, we may give it, share it with another; but beyond that we hardly share anything with another. Sharing implies not only a verbal communication—which is the understanding of the significance of words and their nature—but also communion.

And to commune is one of the most difficult things in life. Perhaps we are fairly good at communicating something which we have or which we want or which we hope to have, but to commune with one another is a most difficult thing.

Because to commune implies, does it not, that both the person who is speaking and the one who is listening must have an intensity, a fury, and that there must be at the same level, at the same time, a state of mind that is neither accepting nor rejecting but actively listening. Then only is there a possibility of communion, of being in communion with something. To be in communion with nature is comparatively easy. And you can be in communion with something when there is no barrier—verbal, intellectual—between you, the observer, and the thing that is observed. But there is a state, perhaps, of affection, a state of intensity, so that both meet at the same level, at the same time, with the same intensity. Otherwise communication is not possible—especially communion which is actually the sharing. And this act of communion is really quite remarkable because it is that communion, that state of intensity, that really transforms one's whole state of mind.

After all, love—if I may use that word without giving to it any particular significance now—is only possible when there is the act of sharing. And that is only possible, again, when there is this peculiar quality of intensity, nonverbal communication, at the same level and at the same time. Otherwise it is not love. Otherwise it becomes mere emotionalism and sentimentalism, which is absolutely worthless.

Our everyday life—not the supreme moment of a second, but everyday life—is this act of imparting, listening, and understanding. And for most of us, listening is one of the most difficult things to do. It is a great art, far greater than any other art. We hardly ever listen because most of us are so occupied with our own problems, with our own ideas, opinions—the everlasting chattering of one's own inadequacies, fancies, myths, and ambitions. One hardly ever pays attention, not only to what another says, but to the birds, to the sunset, to the reflection on the water. One hardly ever sees or listens. And if one knows how to listen—which demands an astonishing energy—then in that act of listening there is complete communion; the words, the significance of words, and the construction of words have very little meaning. So, you and the speaker have completely to share in the truth or in the falseness of what is being said. For most of us, it is a very difficult act to listen; but it is only in listening that one learns.

## — 10 —
## *A Friend or Lover Is Not Just a Piece of Furniture*

Relationship based on mutual need brings only conflict.

However interdependent we are on each other, we are using each other for a purpose, for an end. With an end in view, relationship is not. You may use me and I may use you. In this usage, we lose contact. A society based on mutual usage is the foundation of violence. When we use another, we have only the picture of the end to be gained. The end, the gain, prevents relationship, communion. In the usage of another, however gratifying and comforting it may be, there is always fear. To avoid this fear, we must possess. From this possession there arises envy, suspicion, and constant conflict. Such a relationship can never bring about happiness.

A society whose structure is based on mere need, whether physiological or psychological, must breed conflict, confusion, and misery. Society is the projection of yourself in relation with another, in which the need and the use are predominant.

When you use another for your need, physically or psychologically, in actuality there is no relationship at all; you really have no contact with the other, no communion with the other. How can you have communion with the other when the other is used as a piece of furniture, for your convenience and comfort? So, it is essential to understand the significance of relationship in daily life.

## — 11 —
## *To Be Loved and to Love*

Is it not very important, while we are young, to be loved and to love? It seems to me that most of us neither love nor are loved. And I think it is essential, while we are young, to understand this problem very seriously because it may be that while we are young, we can be sensitive enough to feel it, to know its quality, to know its perfume and perhaps, when we grow older, it will not be entirely destroyed. So, let us consider the question—that is, not that you should not be loved, but that you should love. What does it mean? Is it an ideal? Is it something far away, unattainable? Or is it something that can be felt by each one at odd moments of the day? To feel it, to be aware, to know the quality of sympathy, the quality of understanding, to help naturally, to aid another without any motive, to be kind, to be generous, to have sympathy, to care for something, to care for a dog, to be sympathetic to the villager, to be generous to your friend, to be forgiving, is that what we mean by love? Or is love something in which there is no sense of resentment, something which is everlasting forgiveness? And is it not possible while we are young, to feel it? Most of us, while we are young, do feel it—a sense of outward agony, sympathy to the villager, to the dog, to those who are little. And should it not be constantly tended?

Should you not always have some part of the day when you are helping another or tending a tree or garden or helping in the house or in the hostel so that as you grow into maturity, you will know what it is to be considerate naturally—not with an enforced considerateness that is merely a negative word for one's own happiness, but with that considerateness that is without motive. So, should you not when you are young, know this quality of real affection? It cannot be brought into being; you have to have it, and those who are in charge of you, like your guardian, your parents, your teachers, must also have it. Most people have not got it. They are concerned with their achievements, with their longings, with their success, with their knowledge, and with what they have done.

They have built up their past into such colossal importance that it ultimately destroys them. So, should you not, while you are young, know what it is to take care of the rooms, to care for a number of trees that you yourself dig and plant so that there is a feeling, a subtle feeling of sympathy, of care, of generosity, the actual generosity—not the generosity of the mere mind—that means you give to somebody the little that you may have? If that is not so, if you do not feel that while you are young, it will be very difficult to feel that when you are old. So, if you have that feeling of love, of generosity, of kindness, of gentleness, then perhaps you can awaken that in others.

CHAPTER FOUR

# ABSTINENCE AND CHASTITY

— 1 —

### *Abstinence Is Only Control*

Man has always been trying to reach...a state of bliss, of truth... and man has tortured his mind—through discipline, through control, through self-denial, through abstinence, austerity...

All the systems of the East and of the West imply constant control, constant twisting of the mind to conform to a pattern laid down by the priest, by the sacred books, by all those unfortunate things which are of the very essence of violence.

Their violence is not in the denying of the flesh but also in the denial of every form of desire, every form of beauty...

— 2 —

### *Vows of Abstinence Waste Energy, which Does Not Mean Indulge in Sex*

You take a vow...and suppress, control, battle with yourself endlessly all your life, to keep your vow. Look at the waste of energy! It is also a waste of energy to indulge. And it has far more significance when you suppress. The effort that has gone into suppression, into control, into this denial of your desire distorts your mind...

— 3 —

*Abstinence Is Merely Control: Chastity Is Love*

Chastity can exist only when there is love, and without love there is no chastity. Without love, chastity is merely lust in a different form... So, chastity ceases to be a problem where there is love. Then life is not a problem; life is to be lived completely in the fullness of love, and that revolution will bring about a new world.

— 4 —

*When there Is Love, Sex Takes Its Rightful Place*

A disciplined heart, a suppressed heart, cannot know what love is. It cannot know love if it is caught in habit, in sensation—religious or physical, psychological or sensate.... Only when the mind and heart are unburdened of fear, of the routine of sensational habits, when there is generosity and compassion, there is love. Such love is chaste.

CHAPTER FIVE

# MARRIAGE AND FRIENDSHIP

## — 1 —
## *We Are Never at Home with Anybody Because We Are Living in Our Own Thoughts*

We all want companionship, we all want sexual relationships, a biological necessity. And also we want somebody on whom we can rely, in whom we can find security, in whom there is a sense of comfort, support. Because most of us cannot stand alone, on our own feet, therefore we say, I must marry or I will have a friend or whatever it is, I must have somebody with whom I can be at home. We are never at home with anybody because we are living in our own thoughts, in our own problems, in our own ambitions, and so on. We are frightened to stand alone. Because life is very lonely, life is very, very complex and troublesome and one needs somebody with whom you can talk things over. Also, when you marry you have a sexual relationship, children, and so on. In this relationship between man and woman if there is no love, you exploit each other...

So one has to find out how to live with another without any conflict.... That requires a great deal of intelligence, integrity.

## — 2 —
## *Relation Means to Be in Contact*

The word means to be in contact, to have a sense of wholeness with another, not as separate entities coming together and feeling whole, but the very relationship brings about this quality, this feeling of not being separate...

Are we ever related in the deep, profound sense of that word? Can there be a relationship of that kind, undisturbed like the depth of the sea?...

## — 3 —
## *The Relationship Is a Flowering Thing*

So if I have this quality of mind, brain, or feeling that relationship is a flowering, a movement—it is not a static state, it is a living thing, you can't put it in a crate and say that is it, and not move from there—then we can begin to ask: what is marriage? Right? Or not marriage; one may live with another, sexually, as companions, holding hands, talking... Responsibility is essential—right? I am responsible for the people I live with. I am responsible, not only with my wife, but I am responsible for what is happening in the world...

If I have children, if I love them as I do and I feel responsible, I am responsible for the whole of their lives, and they must be responsible for me for the whole of their lives.

I must see that they are properly educated, not butchered by war...

Unless one has this quality of love everything is just beside the point.

## — 4 —
## *There Is No Love in Habit*

It is only for the very, very few who love that the married relationship has significance, and then it is unbreakable, then it is not mere habit or convenience, nor is it based on biological, sexual need. In that love which is unconditional the identities are fused...

But for most of you, the married relationship is not fused....You live in your isolation, and they live in their isolation, and you have established your habits of assured sexual pleasure...

Love is not habitual; love is something joyous, creative, new. Therefore habit is the contrary of love, but you are caught in habit, and naturally your habitual relationship with another is dead....Therefore, you as a responsible individual in relationship have to do something...and you can act only when there is an awakening of your mind and heart.

## — 5 —
## *Surely, It Must Be Possible to Function in a Sexual Relationship with Someone You Love without the Nightmare Which Usually Follows*

Can't two people be in love and both be so intelligent and so sensitive that there is freedom and absence of a center that makes for conflict? Conflict is not the feeling of being in love. The feeling of being in love is utterly without conflict. There is no loss of energy in being in love. The loss of energy is in the tail, in everything that follows—jealousy, possessiveness, suspicion, doubt, the fear of losing that love, the constant demand for reassurance and security. Surely, it must be possible to function in a sexual relationship with someone you love without the nightmare which usually follows. Of course it is.

CHAPTER SIX

# TEACHERS, SCHOOL, EDUCATION, AND YOU

## — 1 —

### *Why Are You Being Educated?*

Have you ever thought why you are being educated, why you are learning history, mathematics, geography or what else? Have you ever thought why you go to schools and colleges? Is it not very important to find out why you are being crammed with information, with knowledge? What is all this so-called education? Your parents send you here, perhaps because they themselves have passed certain examinations and taken various degrees. Have you ever asked yourselves why you are here, and have the teachers asked you why you are here? Do the teachers know why they are here? Should you not try to find out what all this struggle is about—this struggle to study, to pass examinations, to live in a certain place away from home and not be frightened, to play games well, and so on? Should your teachers not help you to inquire into all this and not merely prepare you to pass examinations?

Do you see all this? Are you not aware of it in your family, in your neighborhood? Have you noticed how it goes on all the time? Must you not find out what is the meaning of education, why you want to be educated, why your parents want you to be educated, why they make elaborate speeches about what education is supposed to be doing in the world?

You may be able to read Bernard Shaw's plays, you may be able to quote Shakespeare or Voltaire or some new philosopher; but if you in yourself are not intelligent, if you are not creative, what is the point of this education?

So, is it not important for the teachers as well as for the students to find out how to be intelligent? Education does not consist in merely being able to read and pass examinations; any clever person can do that. Education consists in cultivating intelligence, does it not? By intelligence I do not mean cunning, or trying to be clever in order to outdo somebody else. Intelligence, surely, is something quite different. There is intelligence when you are not afraid. And when are you afraid? Fear comes when you think of what people may say about you, or what your parents may say; you are afraid of being criticized, of being punished, of failing to pass an examination.

When your teacher scolds you, or when you are not popular in your class, in your school, in your surroundings, fear gradually creeps in.

Fear is obviously one of the barriers to intelligence, is it not? And surely it is the very essence of education to help the student—you and me—to be aware of and to understand the causes of fear, so that from childhood onwards he can live free of fear.

## — 2 —
## *True Education Helps You to Understand Life, not Just Achieve Rewards*

The right kind of education is concerned with individual freedom, which alone can bring true cooperation with the whole, with the many; but this freedom is not achieved through the pursuit of one's own aggrandizement and success. Freedom comes with self-knowledge, when the mind goes above and beyond the hindrances it has created for itself through craving its own security.

It is the function of education to help each individual to discover all these psychological hindrances, and not merely impose upon him new patterns of conduct, new modes of thought. Such impositions will never awaken intelligence, creative understanding, but will only further condition the individual. Surely, this is what is happening throughout the world, and that is why our problems continue and multiply.

It is only when we begin to understand the deep significance of human life that there can be true education; but to understand, the mind must intelligently free itself from the desire for reward which breeds fear and conformity. If we regard our children as personal property, if to us they are the continuance of our petty selves and the fulfillment of our ambitions, then we shall build an environment, a social structure in which there is no love, but only the pursuit of self-centered advantages.

## — 3 —
## *Right Education*

The right kind of education is not possible. To study each child requires patience, alertness, and intelligence. To observe the child's tendencies, aptitudes, temperament, to understand their difficulties, to take into account their heredity and parental influence and not merely regard them as belonging to a certain category—all this calls for a swift and pliable mind, untrammeled by any system or prejudice. It calls for skill, intense interest and, above all, a sense of affection; and to produce educators endowed with these qualities is one of our major problems today.

The spirit of individual freedom and intelligence should pervade the whole school at all times. This can hardly be left to chance, and the casual mention at odd moments of the words and has very little significance. It is particularly important that students and teachers meet regularly to discuss all matters relating to the well-being of the whole group. A student council should be formed, on which the teachers are represented, which can thrash out all the problems of discipline, cleanliness, food, and so on, and which can also help to guide any students who may be somewhat self-indulgent, indifferent, or obstinate.

The students should choose from among themselves those who are to be responsible for the carrying out of decisions and for helping with the general supervision. After all, self-government in the school is a preparation for self-government in later life. If, while they are at school, the child learns to be considerate, impersonal, and intelligent in any discussion pertaining to their daily problems, when they are older they will be able to meet effectively and dispassionately the greater and more complex trials of life. The school should encourage children to understand one another's difficulties and peculiarities, moods and tempers; for then, as they grow up, they will be more thoughtful and patient in their relationship with others.

This same spirit of freedom and intelligence should be evident also in the child's studies. If they are to be creative and not merely an automaton, the student should not be encouraged to accept formulas and conclusions. Even in the study of a science, one should reason with them, helping them to see the problem in its entirety and to use their own judgment.

If the educator is concerned with the freedom of the individual, and not with their own preconceptions, they will help the child to discover that freedom by encouraging them to understand their own environment, their own temperament, their religious and family background, with all the influences and effects they can possibly have on them.

## — 4 —
## *Discover Your Own Interests*

The right kind of education should also help the student to discover what they are most interested in. If they do not find their true vocation, all their life will seem wasted; they will feel frustrated doing something which they do not want to do. If they want to be an artist and instead become a clerk in some office, they will spend their life grumbling and pining away. So it is important for each one to find out what they want to do, and then to see if it is worth doing.

Right education should help the student, not only to

develop their capacities, but to understand their own highest interest. In a world torn by wars, destruction and misery, one must be able to build a new social order and bring about a different way of living.

The responsibility for building a peaceful and enlightened society rests chiefly with the educator, and it is obvious, without becoming emotionally stirred up about it, that they have a very great opportunity to help in achieving that social transformation. The right kind of education does not depend on the regulations of any government or the methods of any particular system; it lies in our own hands, in the hands of the parents and the teachers.

If parents really cared for their children, they would build a new society; but fundamentally most parents do not care, and so they have no time for this most urgent problem. They have time for making money, for amusements, for rituals and worship, but no time to consider what is the right kind of education for their children. This is a fact that the majority of people do not want to face. To face it might mean that they would have to give up their amusements and distractions, and certainly they are not willing to do that. So they send their children off to schools where the teacher cares no more for them than they do. Why should they care? Teaching is merely a job to them, a way of earning money.

The world we have created is so superficial, so artificial, so ugly if one looks behind the curtain; and we decorate the curtain, hoping that everything will somehow come right.

Most people are unfortunately not very earnest about life except, perhaps, when it comes to making money, gaining power, or pursuing sexual excitement. They do not want to face the other complexities of life, and that is why, when their children grow up, they are as immature and unintegrated as their parents, constantly battling with themselves and with the world.

We say so easily that we love our children; but is there love in our hearts when we accept the existing social conditions, when we do not want to bring about a fundamental transformation in this destructive society? And as long as we look to the specialists to educate our children, this confusion and misery will continue; for the specialists, being concerned with the part and not with the whole, are themselves unintegrated.

Instead of being the most honored and responsible occupation, education is now considered slightingly, and most educators are fixed in a routine. They are not really concerned with integration and intelligence, but with the imparting of information; and someone who merely imparts information with the world crashing about them is not an educator.

An educator is not merely a giver of information; they point the way to wisdom, to truth. Truth is far more important than the teacher....To create a new society, each one of us has to be a true teacher, which means that we have to be both the pupil and the master; we have to educate ourselves.

## — 5 —
## *Freedom from Conditioning and Conforming*

The child is the repository of influence, are they not? They are being influenced, not only by you and me, but by their environment, by their school, by the climate, by the food they eat, by the books they read. If their parents are Catholics or communists, they are deliberately shaped, conditioned, and this is what every parent, every teacher does in different ways. And can we be aware of these multiplying influences and help the child to be aware of them, so that as they grow up they will not be caught in any one of them? So what is important, surely, is to help the child as they mature, not to be conditioned as a Christian, as a Hindu, or an Australian, but to be a totally intelligent human being, and this can take place only if you as the teacher or the parent see the truth that there must be freedom from the very beginning.

Freedom is not the outcome of discipline. Freedom does not come after conditioning the mind or while conditioning is going on. There can be freedom only if you and I are aware of all the influences that condition the mind and help the child to be equally aware, so that they do not become entangled in any of them. But most parents and teachers feel that the child must conform to society. What will they do if they do not conform? To most people conformity is imperative, essential, is it not? We have accepted the idea that the child must adjust themselves to the civilization, the culture, the society about them. We take this for granted, and through education we help the child to conform, to adjust themselves to society.

But is it necessary that the child should adjust themselves to society? If the parent or the teacher feels that freedom is the imperative, the essential thing, and not mere conformity to society, then as the child grows up, they will be aware of the influences that condition the mind and will not conform to the present society with its greed, its corruption, its force, its dogmas and authoritarian outlook; and such people will create a totally different kind of society.

We say that someday there is going to be a Utopia. Theoretically it is very nice, but it does not come into existence, and I am afraid the educator needs educating, as the parent does. If we are only concerned with conditioning the child to conform to a particular culture or pattern of society, then we shall perpetuate the present state with its everlasting battle between ourselves and others and continue in the same misery.

CHAPTER SEVEN

# PARENTS, SOCIETY, AND YOU

## — 1 —
## *What Do Parents Really Want?*

It is generally understood that parents desire their children to be educated to fit into society, to adjust themselves and adapt their thoughts into society, which really means helping them to prepare for a profession of some kind so that they can earn a livelihood. They want their children to be educated to pass examinations, to take a degree at some university, and then to have a fairly good job, a secure position in society. That is all most parents are concerned with.

That brings up the complex question of what is the cultural or social background of the parent and the educator, does it not? It means, really, investigating to find out what society is, and whether education is merely a matter of conditioning the child to serve society according to the established pattern.

On the other hand, when they grow up and leave university, should the student be in opposition to society? Or should they be capable of creating a new kind of society altogether? As parents, what is it we want?

## — 2 —
## *Social Purpose of Education*

*Comment*: There is one thing we don't want—that a young person who has had a good education in an expensive school should just demand comforts from society. Such people give nothing in return, and they are impoverishing the country.

*Krishnamurti*: That is, how can education help the student, from childhood right through adolescence to maturity, not to be antisocial?...when we talk of educating them not to be antisocial, we also mean conditioning them not to break out of the established pattern. As long as they conform and stay within the pattern of society, we call them a social asset, but the moment they break away from the pattern we say they are antisocial.

So, is it the function of education merely to mold the student to fit into a particular society? Or should education help them to understand what society is, with its corrupting, destructive, disintegrating factors, so that they comprehend the whole process and step out of it? The stepping out of it is not antisocial. On the contrary, not to conform to any given society is the true social action.

## — 3 —
## *What Is the Relationship between Parent and Child?*

If I am a parent, what is my relationship with my child? First of all, have I any relationship at all? The child happens to be my son or my daughter, but is there actually any relationship, any contact, companionship, communion between myself and my child, or am I too busy earning money, or whatever it is, and therefore pack them off to school? So I really have no contact or communion at all with the boy or the girl, have I? If I am a busy parent, as parents generally are, and I merely want my children to be something, a lawyer, a doctor, or an engineer, have I any relationship with them even though I have produced them?

*Questioner*: I feel I ought to have a relationship with my child, and I am hoping to establish one on which they can depend. How am I to proceed?

*Krishnamurti*: We are discussing the relationship of the parent with their child, and we are asking ourselves if there is any relationship at all, though we say there is. What is that relationship? You have produced the child and you want them to pass through college, but have you actually any other relationship with them? The very rich man has his amusements, his worries, and he has no time for the child, so he sees them occasionally, and when the child is eight or ten years old, he packs them off to school, and that is the end of it. The middle class are also much too busy to have any relationship with the child, they have to go to the office every day, and the poor man's relationship with the child is work, for the child must also work.

## — 4 —
## *Parents Who Love, Change, So Their Children Can Change*

So, let us establish what the word means in our life. What is the relationship between myself and society? After all, society is relationship, is it not? And if I really had a feeling of deep love for my child, that very love would create quite a revolution because I would not want my child to fit into society and have all his initiative destroyed, I would not want them weighed down by tradition, by fear and corruption, bowing to the highly-placed and kicking the lowly. I would see to it that this decaying society ceased to exist, that wars and every form of violence came to an end. Surely, if we love our children, it means that we must find a way of educating them so that they do not merely fit into society.

So, what is the function of education? Is it not to help the student to understand their own compulsions, motives, urges, which create the pattern of a destructive society? Is it not to help them to understand and break through their own conditionings, their own limitations?

*Comment*: I think it is first necessary for the child to understand the society in which they are; otherwise, they cannot break away from it.

*Krishnamurti*: They are part of society, they are in contact with it every day and sees its corruption. Now, how are you going to help them, through education, to understand the implications of this society and be free of it so that they can create a different kind of social order?

## — 5 —
## *Parents as Teachers Need Education*

*Comment*: A common child inevitably conforms to the pattern of society.

*Krishnamurti*: There is no such thing as a common child, but there may be a common teacher who is scared stiff. That is why the educator needs educating. They also must change and not merely conform to society.

## — 6 —
## *Young People Are Not the Problem*

The right kind of education begins with the educator, who must understand themselves and be free from established patterns of thought; for what they are, that they impart. If they have not been rightly educated, what can they teach except the same mechanical knowledge on which they themselves have been brought up? The problem, therefore, is not the child, but the parent and the teacher; the problem is to educate the educator.

If we who are the educators do not understand ourselves, if we do not understand our relationship with the child but merely stuff them with information and make them pass examinations, how can we possibly bring about a new kind of education? The pupil is there to be guided and helped; but if the guide, the helper are themselves confused and narrow, nationalistic and theory-ridden, then naturally their pupil will be what they are, and education becomes a source of further confusion and strife...

To be concerned with our own re-education is far more necessary than to worry about the future well-being and security of the child.

## — 7 —
## *Are We Taught How to Think—or What to Think?*

To educate the educator—that is, to have them understand themselves—is one of the most difficult undertakings, because most of us are already crystallized within a system of thought or a pattern of action; we have already given ourselves over to some ideology, to a religion, or to a particular standard of conduct. That is why we teach the child what to think and not how to think.

Moreover, parents and teachers are largely occupied with their own conflicts and sorrows. Rich or poor, most parents are absorbed in their personal worries and trials. They are not gravely concerned about the present social and moral deterioration, but only desire that their children shall be equipped to get on in the world. They are anxious about the future of their children, eager to have them educated to hold secure positions, or to marry well.

Contrary to what is generally believed, most parents do not love their children, though they talk of loving them. If parents really loved their children, there would be no emphasis laid on the family and the nation as opposed to the whole, which creates social and racial divisions between men and brings about war and starvation. It is really extraordinary that, while people are rigorously trained to be lawyers or doctors, they may become parents without undergoing any training whatsoever to fit them for this all-important task.

More often than not, the family, with its separate tendencies, encourages the general process of isolation, thereby becoming a deteriorating factor in society. It is only when there is love and understanding that the walls of isolation are broken down, and then the family is no longer a closed circle, it is neither a prison nor a refuge; then the parents are in communion, not only with their children, but also with their neighbors.

Being absorbed in their own problems, many parents shift to the teacher the responsibility for the well-being of their children; and then it is important that the educator help in the education of the parents as well.

The educator must talk to them, explaining that the confused state of the world mirrors their own individual confusion. They must point out that scientific progress in itself cannot bring about a radical change in existing values; that technical training, which is now called education, has not given man freedom or made him any happier; and that to condition the student to accept the present environment is not conducive to intelligence. They must tell them what they are attempting to do for their child, and how they are setting about it. They have to awaken the parents' confidence, not by assuming the authority of a specialist dealing with ignorant laymen, but by talking over with them the child's temperament, difficulties, aptitudes, and so on.

If the teacher takes a real interest in the child as an individual, the parents will have confidence in them. In this process, the teacher is educating the parents as well as themselves, while learning from them in return. Right education is a mutual task demanding patience, consideration and affection.

## — 8 —
## *Do We Really Love Our Children?*

Do parents ever ask themselves why they have children? Do they have children to perpetuate their name, to carry on their property? Do they want children merely for the sake of their own delight, to satisfy their own emotional needs? If so, then the children become a mere projection of the desires and fears of their parents. Can parents claim to love their children when, by educating them wrongly, they foster envy, enmity, and ambition? Is it love that stimulates the national and racial antagonisms which lead to war, destruction and utter misery, that sets man against man in the name of religions and ideologies?

Many parents encourage their children in the ways of

conflict and sorrow, not only by allowing them to be submitted to the wrong kind of education, but by the manner in which they conduct their own lives; and then, when the children grow up and suffer, the parents pray for them or find excuses for their behavior. The suffering of parents for their children is a form of possessive self-pity which exists only when there is no love.

If parents love their children, they will not be nationalistic, they will not identify themselves with any country; for the worship of the state brings on war, which kills or maims their sons. If parents love their children, they will discover what is right relationship to property; for the possessive instinct has given property an enormous and false significance which is destroying the world. If parents love their children, they will not belong to any organized religion; for dogma and belief divide people into conflicting groups, creating antagonism between man and man. If parents love their children, they will do away with envy and strife, and will set about altering fundamentally the structure of present-day society.

## — 9 —
## *The Awakening of Intelligence in Parent and Child*

We should not continue to fit thoughtlessly into the pattern in which we happen to have been brought up. How can there ever be harmony in the individual and so in society if we do not understand ourselves? Unless the educator understands themselves, unless they see their own conditioned responses and are beginning to free themselves from existing values, how can they possibly awaken intelligence in the child? And if they cannot awaken intelligence in the child, then what is their function?

It is only by understanding the ways of our own thought and feeling that we can truly help the child to be a free human being; and if the educator is vitally concerned with this, they will be keenly aware, not only of the child, but also of themselves.

CHAPTER EIGHT

# RELATIONSHIP TO ONESELF

## — 1 —
## *What Are You Looking For?*

So it seems to me very important to find out what it is we are seeking. This is not a rhetorical question but a question that each one of us must inevitably put to ourselves; and the more mature, intelligent, and alert we are, the greater and more urgent our demand to find out what it is that we are seeking.

Unfortunately most of us put this question superficially, and when we receive a superficial answer, we are satisfied with it. But if you care to go into the matter, you will find that the mind is merely seeking some kind of satisfaction, some kind of pleasant invention which will gratify it; and once having found or created for itself a shelter of opinion and conclusion, therein it stays, so our search seemingly comes to an end. Or if we are dissatisfied, we go from one philosophy to another, from one dogma to another, from one church, from one sect, from one book to another, always trying to find a permanent security, inwardly as well as outwardly, a permanent happiness, a permanent peace.

## — 2 —
## *Understand the Mind, the Self, that Is Searching*

Before we begin to seek, then, is it not important to understand the process of the mind itself? Because what we are seeking now is fairly obvious.... To understand oneself needs enormous patience because the self is a very complex process, and if one does not understand oneself, whatever one seeks will have very little significance. When we do not understand our own urges and compulsions, conscious as well as unconscious, they produce certain activities which create conflict in ourselves; and what we are seeking is to avoid or escape from this conflict, is it not? So, as long as we do not understand the process of ourselves, of our own thinking, our search is extremely superficial, narrow, and petty.

## — 3 —
## *Self-Knowledge Is the Key to Freedom*

So, if we really want to create a different world, a different relationship between human beings, a different attitude toward life, it is essential that we should first understand ourselves, is it not? This does not mean self-centered concentration, which leads to utter misery. What I am suggesting is that without self-knowledge, without deeply knowing oneself, all inquiry, all thought, all conclusions, opinions, and values have very little meaning. Most of us are conditioned—conditioned as Christians, as Muslims, or what you will, and within that narrow area we have our being. Our minds are conditioned by society, by education, by the culture about us, and without understanding the total process of that conditioning, our search, our knowledge, our inquiry can only lead to further mischief, to greater misery, which is what is actually happening.

Self-knowledge is not according to any formula. You may go to a psychologist, or a psychoanalyst to find out about yourself, but that is not self-knowledge. Self-knowledge comes into being when we are aware of ourselves in relationship, which shows what we are from moment to moment.

## — 4 —
## *Relationship and Isolation*

I have said that one can discover oneself only in relationship. That is so, is it not? One cannot know oneself, what one actually is except in relationship. Anger, jealousy, envy, lust—all such reactions exist only in one's relationship with people, with things, and with ideas. If there is no relationship at all, if there is complete isolation, one cannot know oneself. The mind can isolate itself, thinking that it is somebody, which is a state of lunacy, unbalance, and in that state it cannot know itself. It merely has ideas about itself, like the idealist who is isolating himself from the fact of what he is by pursuing what he should be. That is what most of us are doing. Because relationship is painful, we want to isolate ourselves from this pain, and in the isolating process we create the ideal of what we should be, which is imaginary, an invention of the mind.

So we can know ourselves as we actually are, consciously as well as unconsciously, only in relationship, and that is fairly obvious.

I hope you are interested in all this because it is part of our daily activity; it is our very life, and if we do not understand it, merely going to a series of meetings or acquiring knowledge from books will have very little meaning.

## — 5 —
## *Is There a Self without Relationship?*

The second part of the question is this: "Is the self an isolated reality, or is there no self at all without relationship?" In other words, do I exist only in relationship, or do I exist as an isolated reality beyond relationship? I think the latter is what most of us would like because relationship is painful. In the very fulfillment of relationship, there is fear, anxiety; and knowing this, the mind seeks to isolate itself with its gods, its higher self, and so on. The very nature of the self, the 'me', is a process of isolation, is it not? The self and the concerns of the self—my family, my property, my love, my desire—is a process of isolation, and this process is a reality in the sense that it is actually taking place. And can such a self-enclosed mind ever find something beyond itself? Obviously not. It may stretch its walls, its boundaries; it may expand its area, but it is still the consciousness of the 'me'.

## — 6 —
## *Conflict and Pain Keep the 'Me' Alive*

Now, when do you know you are related? Are you conscious of being related when there is complete unanimity, when there is love? Or does the consciousness of being related arise only when there is friction, when there is conflict, when you are demanding something, when there is frustration, fear, contention between the 'me' and the other who is related to the 'me'? Does the sense of self in relationship exist if you are not in pain? Let us look at it much more simply.

If you are not in pain, do you know that you exist? Say, for instance, you are happy for a moment. At the precise moment of experiencing happiness, are you aware that you are happy? Surely, it is only a second afterwards that you become conscious that you are happy. And is it not possible for the mind to be free from all self-enclosing demands and pursuits so that the self is not? Then perhaps relationship can have quite a different meaning. Relationship now is used as a means of security, as a means of self-perpetuation, self-expansion, self-aggrandizement. All these qualities make up the self, and if they cease, then there may be another state in which relationship has a different significance altogether.

After all, most relationship is now based on envy because envy is the basis of our present culture, and therefore in our relationship with each other, which is society, there is contention, violence, a constant battle. But if there is no envy at all, neither conscious nor unconscious, neither superficial nor deep-rooted, if all envy has totally ceased, then is not our relationship entirely different?

## — 7 —
## *Is there a State of Mind Not Bound by the Self?*

So is there a state of mind which is not bound by the idea of the self? Please, this is not a theory; it is not some philosophy to be practiced. But if you are really listening to what is being said, you are bound to experience the truth of it.

## — 8 —
## *Self-Knowledge Is the Means to Approaching Psychological, Social, Economic Problems*

So it seems to me that to understand a problem requires not a ready-made answer, not trying to seek a solution for the problem, but a direct consideration of the problem itself, which is to approach it without the desire to find an answer, if one may so put it. Then you are directly in relationship with the problem, then you are the problem; the problem is no longer separate from yourself. And I think that is the first thing one must realize—that the problem of existence, with all its complexities, is not different from ourselves. We are the problem, and as long as we regard the problem as something away from us, or apart from us, our approach must inevitably result in failure. Whereas, if we can regard the problem as our own, as part of us, not separate from us, then perhaps we shall be able to understand it significantly—which means essentially, does it not, that a problem exists because there is no self-knowledge. If I do not understand myself, the whole complexity of myself, I have no basis for thinking. 'Myself' is not at any one particular level, surely. 'Myself' is at all levels, at whatever level I may place it. So, as long as I have no comprehension of myself, as long as I do not understand myself fully, significantly—the conscious as well as the unconscious, the superficial as well as the hidden—obviously I have no means of approaching the problem, whether it be economic, social, psychological, or any other problem.

## — 9 —

## *Self Is the Same in All of Us: Understand Yours, and You Understand the World's Problems*

Self-knowledge is the beginning of the understanding of the problem. Belief, ideas, knowledge have really no significance at all without self-knowledge. Without self-knowledge they lead to illusion, to all kinds of complications and stupidities into which we can so subtly escape—and most of us do.

That is why we join so many societies, so many groups, so many exclusive organizations and secret bodies. Is it not the nature of stupidity to be exclusive? The more one is stupid, the more one is exclusive, religiously or socially; and each exclusiveness creates its own problems.

So, it seems to me, our difficulty in understanding the many problems that confront us, both the subtle and the obvious, comes about through ignorance of ourselves. It is we who create the problem, we who are part of the environment—as well as something more, which we shall discover if we can understand ourselves.

## — 10 —
## *We Seek Permanent Security*

Most of us seek security of some kind because our lives are an endless conflict, from the moment we are born to the moment we die. The boredom of life and the anxiety of life; the despair of existence; the feeling that you want to be loved, and you are not loved; the shallowness, the pettiness, the travail of everyday existence—that is our life. In that life there is danger, there is apprehension; nothing is certain; there is always the uncertainty of tomorrow. So you are all the time pursuing security, consciously or unconsciously; you want to find a permanent state, psychologically first and outwardly afterwards—it is always psychological first, not outward. You want a permanent state where you will not be disturbed by anything, by any fear, by any anxiety, by any sense of uncertainty, by any sense of guilt. That is what most of us want.

That is what most of us seek outwardly as well as inwardly. Outwardly we want very good jobs; we are educated, technologically, to function mechanically in a certain bureaucratic way, or whatever it is. And inwardly we want peace, a sense of certainty, a sense of permanency. In all our relationships, in all our actions, whether we are doing right or wrong, we want to be secure.

## — 11 —
## *Is there Such a Thing as Security?*

First of all, is there such a thing as inward security in relationship, in our affections, in the ways of our thinking? Is there the ultimate reality which every person wants, hopes, pins their faith to? Because the moment you want security, you will invent a god, an idea, an ideal, which will give you the feeling of security; but it may not be real at all—it may be merely an idea, a reaction, a resistance to the obvious fact of uncertainty. So one has to inquire into this question of whether there is security at all at any level of our lives. First, inwardly, because if there is no security outwardly, then our relationship with the world will be entirely different; then we shall not identify ourselves with any group, with any nation, or even with any family.

So, when you put to yourself the question whether there is security or not, the problem becomes extremely complex if you don't understand directly the question, not all the side issues. Because it is the desire to be secure, when there is probably no security at all, that breeds conflict. If psychologically you see the truth that there is no security of any kind, of any type, at any level, there is no conflict. Then, you are creative, volcanic in your action, explosive in your ideas; you are not tethered to anything. Then you are living. And a mind that is in conflict, obviously cannot live clearly with any clarity, with an immense sense of affection and sympathy. To love you must have a mind that is extraordinarily sensitive. But you cannot be sensitive if you are perpetually afraid, perpetually anxious, perpetually worried, insecure, and therefore seeking security. And a mind in conflict, obviously, like any machine that is in friction, is wearing itself out; it becomes dull, stupid, bored.

So, first then, is there such a thing as security? You have to find out, not me. I say there is no security of any kind, psychologically, at any level, at any depth.

Is there security? Is there permanency which man is seeking all the time? As you notice for yourself, your body changes, the cells of the body change so often. As you see for yourself in your relationship with your wife, with your children, with your neighbor, with your state, with your community, is there anything permanent? You would like to make it permanent. The relationship with your wife—you call it marriage, and legally hold it tightly. But is there permanency in that relationship? Because if you have invested permanency in your wife or husband, when she turns away, or looks at another, or dies, or some illness takes place, you are completely lost....

The actual state of every human being is uncertainty. Those who realize the actual state of uncertainty either see the fact and live with it there or they go off, become neurotic, because they cannot face that uncertainty. They cannot live with something that demands an astonishing swiftness of mind and heart, and so they become monks, they adopt every kind of fanciful escape. So you have to see the actual, and not escape in good works, good action, going to the temple, talking. The fact is something demands your complete attention. The fact is that all of us are insecure; there is nothing secure.

## — 12 —
## *Understand Completely this Problem of Security*

For most of us life is empty. Being empty, we try to fill it with all kinds of things. But if you understand this question of security and insecurity, you will find, as you go into it deeper and deeper—I am using the word deeper in the sense of noncomparatively—that it is not a question of time. Then you understand completely this problem of security and conflict.

Then you will find—find, not believe—for yourself a state where there is complete existence, complete being, in which there is no sense of fear, no anxiety, no sense of obedience, compulsion; a complete state of being; a light that does not seek, that has no movement beyond itself.

SECTION TWO

# SOCIETY AND YOUR RELATIONSHIPS

## CHAPTER NINE

# SOCIETY AND YOU

### — 1 —
### *Who Is Society?*

To find the full significance of living, we must understand the daily tortures of our complex life; we cannot escape from them. The society in which we live has to be understood by each one of us—not by some philosopher, not by some teacher, not by a guru—and our way of living has to be transformed, completely changed. I think that is the most important thing we have to do, and nothing else. In the process of transformation, in the process of bringing about, without bargaining, a change in our life, there is beauty; and in that change we shall find for ourselves the great mystery that each mind is seeking. Therefore, we must concern ourselves not with what is beyond life, or what is life, or what is the purpose of life, but rather with the understanding of this complex existence of everyday life, because that is the foundation upon which we must build. And without understanding that, without bringing about a radical change in that, our society will always be in a state of corruption, and therefore, we shall always be in a state of deterioration.

We are society; we are not independent of society. We are the result of the environment—of our religion, of our education, of the climate, of the food we eat, the reactions, the innumerable repetitive activities that we indulge in every day.

That is our life. And the society in which we live is part of that life. Society is relationship between man and man. Society is cooperation. Society, as it is, is the result of man's greed, hatred, ambition, competition, brutality, cruelty, ruthlessness—and we live in that pattern. And to understand it—not intellectually, not merely theoretically, but actually—we have to come into contact directly with that fact, which is, a human being—that is you—is the result of this social environment, its economic pressure, religious upbringing, and so on. To come into contact with anything directly is not to verbalize it but to look at it.

## — 2 —
## *You Are Society*

What you are, the world is. So your problem is the world's problem. Surely, this is a simple and basic fact, is it not? In our relationship with the one or the many we seem somehow to overlook this point all the time. We want to bring about alteration through a system or through a revolution in ideas or values based on a system, forgetting that it is you and I who create society, who bring about confusion or order by the way in which we live. So we must begin near, that is we must concern ourselves with our daily existence, with our daily thoughts and feelings and actions which are revealed in the manner of earning our livelihood and in our relationship with ideas or beliefs. This is our daily existence, is it not? We are concerned with livelihood, getting jobs, earning money; we are concerned with the relationship with our family or with our neighbors, and we are concerned with ideas and with beliefs. Now, if you examine our occupation, it is fundamentally based on envy, it is not just a means of earning a livelihood. Society is so constructed that it is a process of constant conflict, constant becoming; it is based on greed, on envy, envy of your superior; the clerk wanting to become the manager, which shows that he is not just concerned with earning a livelihood, a means of subsistence, but with acquiring position and prestige. This attitude naturally creates havoc in society, in relationship, but if you and I were only concerned with livelihood we should find out the right means of earning it, a means not based on envy. Envy is one of the most destructive factors in relationship because envy indicates the desire for power, for position, and it ultimately leads to politics; both are closely related. The clerk, when he seeks to become a manager, becomes a factor in the creation of power politics which produce war; so he is directly responsible for war.

## — 3 —
## *Society Is the Sum of All Our Relationships*

The process of the individual is not opposed to the world, to the mass, whatever that term may mean, because there is no mass apart from you—you are the mass.

## — 4 —
## *How Does Intelligence Revolt?*

You know, the young people throughout the world are rejecting, revolting against the established order—an order which has made the world ugly, monstrous, chaotic. There have been wars, and for one job, there are thousands of people.

Society has been built by the past generation with its ambitions, its greed, its violence, its ideologies. People, especially the young people, are rejecting all ideologies—perhaps not in this country; for we have not advanced enough, we are not civilized enough to reject all authority, all ideologies. But in rejecting ideologies they are creating their own pattern of ideology: long hair, and all the rest of it.

So, mere revolt does not answer the problem. What answers the problem is to bring about order within oneself, order which is living, not a routine. Routine is deadly. You go to an office the moment you pass out of your college—if you can get a job. Then for the next forty to fifty years, you go to the office every day. You know what happens to such a mind? You have established a routine, and you repeat that routine; and you encourage your child to repeat that routine.

Any man alive must revolt against it. But you will say, "I have responsibility; placed as I am, I cannot leave it even though I would like to." And so the world goes on, repeating the monotony, the boredom of life, its utter emptiness. Against all this, intelligence is revolting.

## — 5 —
## *Making the New Society*

So, there must be a new order, a new way of living. To bring about that new order, that new way of living, we must understand disorder. It is only through negation that you understand the positive, not by the pursuit of the positive.

Do you understand? When you deny, put aside, what is negative; when you understand the whole sociological and inward disorder that human beings have created; when you understand that as long as each human being is ambitious, greedy, invidious, competitive, seeking position, power, authority, he is creating disorder; and when you understand the structure of disorder—that very understanding brings about discipline, discipline not of suppression, not of imitation. Out of negation comes the right discipline, which is order.

## — 6 —
## *Blindly Following Another Destroys You*

There is the so-called authority of the spiritual leaders.... The primary cause of disorder is the pursuit or seeking of a reality which another promises. As most of us are in confusion, as most of us are in turmoil, we would rather mechanically follow somebody who will assure us of a comfortable spiritual life. It is one of the most extraordinary things that politically we are against tyranny, dictatorship. The more liberal, the more civilized, the more free the people are, the more they abhor, they detest tyranny, politically and economically; but inwardly, they would accept the authority, the tyranny of another. That is, we twist our minds, twist our thoughts and our way of life to conform to a certain pattern established by another as the way to reality. When we do that, we are actually destroying clarity, because clarity or light has to be found by oneself, not through another, not through a book, not through any saint.

One cannot deny outward authority. That is necessary. It is essential for any civilized society. But what we are saying is about the authority of another, including the speaker. There can be order only when we understand the disorder that each one of us brings about, because we are part of society; we have created the structure of society, and in that society we are caught. We, as human beings who have inherited animal instincts, have to find, as human beings, light and order. And we cannot find that light and order, or that understanding, through another—it does not matter who it is—because the experiences of another may be false. All experiences must be questioned, whether your own or of another.

— 7 —

## *Reject Even Your Own Conditioning as Authority*

So, one must find out for ourselves why one follows, why one accepts this tyranny of authority—the authority of the priest, the authority of the printed word, the Bible, the Indian scriptures, all the rest of it. Can one reject completely the authority of society? I do not mean the rejection brought about by the beatniks of the world; that is merely a reaction. But can one really see that this outward conformity to a pattern is futile, destructive to the mind that wants to find out what is true, what is real? And if one rejects outer authority, is it possible also to reject the inner, the authority of experience?

Can one put away experience? For most of us, experience is the guidance of knowledge. We say, "I know from experience" or "Experience tells me I must do this" and experience becomes one's inward authority. And perhaps that is far more destructive, far more evil than outward authority. It is the authority of one's conditioning and leads to every form of illusion...

Now, can the mind entirely wipe away the conditioning of centuries? After all, conditioning is of the past. The reactions, the knowledge, the beliefs, the traditions of many thousands of yesterdays have gone to shape the mind. And can it all be wiped away?...

You see, conditioning is the very root of fear; and where there is fear, there is no virtue.

## — 8 —
## *Psychological Security Is a Myth*

I am not going into the unconscious very deeply, I am touching it briefly. The unconscious is the past of many thousands of years. The unconscious is the residue of the race, of the family, the collected knowledge. The unconscious is the whole tradition which you may deny consciously, but it is there. And that becomes our authority in moments when there is trouble. Then the unconscious says: go to church, do this and do that, do puja—whatever you do. The prompting, the hinting of the unconscious with all the past becomes the authority—which becomes our conscience, the inner voice, and all the rest of it. So one has to be aware of all that, understand it and be free of it, in order to find out if there is security, and to live in the truth which you discover for yourself whether there is security or not.

Also we find a great deal of security, psychologically, emotionally, in identifying ourselves with an idea, with a race, with a community, with a particular action. That is, we commit ourselves to a certain cause, to a certain political party, to a certain way of thinking, to certain customs, habits, rituals, as the Hindu, the Parsi, the Christian, the Muslim, and all the rest of it. We commit ourselves to a particular way of thinking; we identify ourselves with a group, with a community, with a particular class, or with a particular idea. This identification with the nation, with the family, with a group, with a community gives you also a certain sense of security.

You feel much more safe when you say "I am an Indian," or "I am an Englishman," or "I am a German," whatever it is... So, first then, is there such a thing as security? You have to find it out, not me. I say there is no security of any kind, psychologically, at any level, at any depth.

# CHAPTER TEN

# WHAT IS TRUE RELIGION?

## — 1 —

## *Religion Has Not Changed Human Behavior*

We said that there must be a radical transformation, a mutation in the mind, because man has tried every method, both outwardly and inwardly, to transform himself. He has gone to temples, churches, mosques; he has tried various political systems, economic order; there is great prosperity and yet there is great poverty. Man in every way—through education, through science, through religion—has tried to bring about a radical mutation in himself. He has gone to a monastery, has given up the world, he has meditated endlessly, repeating prayers, sacrificing, following ideals, pursuing teachers, belonging to various sects. He has tried, if one observes through history, everything he can possibly try to find a way out of this confusion, this misery, this sorrow, this endless conflict. And he has invented a heaven. And in order to avoid hell, which is punishment, he has done also various forms of mental gymnastics, various forms of control; he has tried drugs, sex, innumerable ways that a very clever mind has thought out. And yet man through the world has remained as he was.

## — 2 —
## *Is Belief Religious?*

We realize that life is ugly, painful, sorrowful; we want some kind of theory, some kind of speculation or satisfaction, some kind of doctrine, which will explain all this, and so we are caught in explanation, in words, in theories, and gradually beliefs become deeply rooted and unshakable because behind those beliefs, behind those dogmas, there is the constant fear of the unknown. But we never look at that fear; we turn away from it. The stronger the beliefs, the stronger the dogmas. And when we examine these beliefs—the Christian, the Hindu, the Buddhist—we find that they divide people. Each dogma, each belief has a series of rituals, a series of compulsions which bind man and separate man. So, we start with an inquiry to find out what is true, what the significance is of this misery, this struggle, this pain; and we are soon caught up in beliefs, in rituals, in theories. Belief is corruption because behind belief and morality lurks the mind, the self—the self growing big, powerful and strong. We consider belief in God, the belief in something, as religion. We consider that to believe is to be religious. You understand? If you do not believe, you will be considered an atheist, you will be condemned by society. One society will condemn those who believe in God. And another society will condemn those who do not. They are both the same. So, religion becomes a matter of belief—and belief acts and has a corresponding influence on the mind; the mind then can never be free. But it is only in freedom that you can find out what is true, what is God, not through any belief, because your very belief projects what you think ought to be God, what you think ought to be true.

## — 3 —
## *Religions and Beliefs Separate Us*

You believe in God, and another does not believe in God, so your beliefs separate you from each other. Belief throughout the world is organized as Hinduism, Buddhism, or Christianity, and so it divides man from man. We are confused, and we think that through belief we shall clear the confusion: that is belief is superimposed on the confusion, and we hope that confusion will thereby be cleared away. But belief is merely an escape from the fact of confusion; it does not help us to face and to understand the fact but to run away from the confusion in which we are. To understand the confusion, belief is not necessary. And belief only acts as a screen between ourselves and our problems. So, religion, which is organized belief, becomes a means of escape from, from the fact of confusion. The man who believes in God, the man who believes in the hereafter, or who has any other form of belief, is escaping from the fact of what he is. Do you not know those who believe in God, who do puja, who repeat certain chants and words, and who in their daily life are dominating, cruel, ambitious, cheating, dishonest? Shall they find God? Are they really seeking God? Is God to be found through repetition of words, through belief? But such people believe in God, they worship God, they go to the temple every day, they do everything to avoid the fact of what they are—and such people you consider respectable because they are yourself.

## — 4 —
## *Can True Religion Be Invented by Thought and Its Fears?*

We are concerned with bringing about a different world, a different social order. We are concerned not with religious beliefs and dogmas, superstitions, and rituals but with what is true religion. And to find that out there must be no fear. We see that thought breeds fear, and that thought must be occupied with something, as otherwise it feels itself lost. One of the reasons why we are occupied with God, with social reform, with this, with that, or with something or the other is because in ourselves we are afraid to be lonely, in ourselves we are afraid to be empty. We know what the world is: a world of brutality, ugliness, violence, wars, hatreds, class and national divisions, and so on. Knowing actually what the world is—not what we think it should be—our concern is to bring about a radical transformation in that. To bring about that transformation, the human mind has to undergo tremendous mutation; and the transformation cannot take place if there is any form of fear.

~

Thought is the response of memory which has been accumulated through experience, through knowledge, through tradition; and memory is the result of time, inherited from the animal. And with this background we react. This reaction is thinking. Thought is essential at certain levels. But when thought projects itself as the future and the past psychologically, then thought creates fear as well as pleasure...

Can thought stop thinking about the past psychologically, self-protectively, or about the future?

## — 5 —
## *Complete Attention Wipes Away Fear*

So to be free of fear, give complete attention. Next time fear arises in your mind—fear of what is going to happen, or fear that something that has happened might come back again—give your complete attention; do not run away from it, don't try to change it, don't try to control it, don't try to suppress it, be with it totally, completely, with complete attention. Then you will see that because there is no observer, there is no fear at all...and if you give attention at any moment completely, then you will wipe away the unconscious as well as the limited consciousness.

## — 6 —
## *Can the Mind Come upon the Sacred Without the Rituals Created by Thought?*

Now, how does one come upon it? You understand my question? We have meditated, sacrificed, remained a celibate or not celibate; we have accepted traditions, rituals; we have got tremendously excited over perfume, idols; we have gone round the temples several times and prostrated—we have done all those childish things. And if we have done all that, we have seen the utter futility of all that because they are born out of fear, born out of the sense of wanting some hope, because most of us are in despair. But to be free of despair is not through hope. To be free of despair, you have to understand despair itself, and not introduce the idea of hope. It is very important to understand this because then you create a duality, and there is no end to the corridor of duality.

So, we come to the point: can the mind come upon it without discipline, without thought, without enforcement, without any book, without any leader, without any teacher, without anything? Can the mind come upon it as you come upon that lovely sunset? When can one come upon it? Not the machinery which will make you come upon it—then, it is just another trick.

It seems to me there are certain absolute things that are necessary—not something to be gained, something you practice, something you do day after day. That is, there must be passion without motive. You understand? Passion which is not the result of some commitment or attachment or a motive, because without passion you cannot see beauty. Not the beauty of a sunset like that, not the beauty of a structure, beauty of a poem, beauty of a bird on the wing, but a beauty that is not an intellectual, comparative, social thing. And to come upon that beauty there must be passion. To have that passion there must be love. Just listen. You cannot do a thing about all this; you cannot practice love—then it becomes mere kindliness, generosity, gentleness, a state of nonviolence, peace; but it has nothing whatsoever to do with love. And without passion and beauty, there is no love. Just listen to it.

Don't argue, don't discuss "how?"

It is like leaving a door open. If you leave the door open, the breeze of an evening comes in. You cannot invite it: you cannot prepare for it; you cannot say, "I must, I must not"; you cannot go to rituals and so on; but just leave the door open. This means a very simple act, an act which is not of the will, which is not of pleasure, which is not projected by a cunning mind. Just to leave the door open—that is all you can do; you cannot do anything else. You cannot sit down to meditate, to make the mind silent by force, by compulsion, by discipline. Such a silence is noise and endless misery. All that you can do is to leave the door of your mind open. And you cannot leave that door open if you are not free. So you begin to disentangle yourself from all the stupid psychological inventions that the mind has created—to be free from all that, not in order to leave the door open, but just to be free. It is like keeping a room clean, tidy, and orderly; that is all. Then when you leave the door open without any intention, without any purpose, without any motive, without any longing, then through that door comes something which cannot be measured by time or by experience; it is not related to any activity of the mind. Then you will know for yourself, beyond all doubt, that there is something far beyond all the imagination of man, beyond time, beyond all inquiry.

CHAPTER ELEVEN

# GOVERNMENT, ARMY, AND THE LAW

## — 1 —

### *Will Authority Transform the Human Mind?*

Will authority transform the human mind? This is very important to understand because to us authority is very important. Though we may revolt against authority, we set up our own authority...

There is the authority of the law, which obviously one must accept. Then there is the psychological authority, the authority of one who knows, as the priest. Nobody bothers about the priest nowadays. The so-called intellectual, fairly clear-thinking people, don't care about the priest, the church, and all their inventions, but they have their own authority, which is the authority of the intellect, reason, or knowledge, and they follow that authority. A man afraid, uncertain, not clear in his activities, in his life, wants some authority to tell him what to do—the authority of the analyst, the book, or the latest fad.

Can the mind be free from authority, which means free from fear, so that it is no longer capable of following? If so, this puts an end to imitation, which becomes mechanical.

After all, virtue, ethics, is not a repetition of what is good.

The moment it becomes mechanical, it ceases to be virtue.

Virtue is something that must be from moment to moment, like humility. Humility cannot be cultivated, and a mind that has no humility is incapable of learning. So virtue has no authority.

The social morality is no morality at all; it's immoral because it admits competition, greed, ambition, and therefore society is encouraging immorality.

— 2 —

*Government Law, the Army, and Killing*

*Comment*: Earlier you said that we must accept the authority of law. I can understand this with respect to such things as traffic regulations, but the law would have me become a soldier, and that I cannot accept.

*Krishnamurti*: This is a problem all over the world. Governments demand that you join the army, take some kind of part in war. What are you going to do, especially when you are young? We older people are finished. What happens to the young people? This is a question that is asked everywhere in the world.

Now, there is no authority. I'm not advising what you should do or not do, whether you should join or not join, should kill or not kill. We are examining the question.

In India at one time in the past there was a community within that society which said, "We will not kill." They didn't kill animals for their food. They thought a great deal of not hurting another, speaking kindly, having always a certain respect for virtue. That community existed for many, many centuries. It was especially in the south as the Brahmin. But all that's gone. What are you to do: to help war or not to help? When you buy a stamp, you are helping the war; when you pay a tax, you are helping the war; when you earn money, you are helping the war; when you are working in a factory, you are producing shells for the war; and the way you live, with your competition, ambition, self-centered prosperity, you are producing war. When the government asks that you join the army, either you decide that you must, or must not and face all the consequences. I know a boy in Europe. There every boy must go through the army for a year, or a year and a half, or two years. This boy said, "I don't want to do it. I'm not going to do it." And he said, "I am going to run away." And he ran away, which means that he can never come back to his country. He left his property with the family. He can never see his family again. Whether you decide to join or not to join becomes a very small affair when there are much larger issues concerned.

## — 3 —
## *Man Has Chosen the Way of War*

The larger issue is how to stop wars altogether, not this particular war or that particular war. You have your favorite war, and I may have my favorite war. Because I may happen to be a British citizen and hate Hitler, therefore I fight him; but I don't fight the Vietnamese because it's not my favorite war; it doesn't pay me politically, or whatever the reasons may be. The larger issue is: man has chosen the way of war, conflict. Unless you alter that totally, you will be caught in this question in which the questioner is caught. To alter that totally, completely, you must live peacefully, not killing, either by word or by deed. That means no competition, no division of sovereign governments, no army. You say, "It is impossible for me to do it; I can't stop the war; I can't stop the army." But what is important, it seems to me, is that when you see the whole structure of human violence and brutality, which expresses itself ultimately in war, if you see that totally, then in the very act of seeing, you will do the right thing. The right thing may produce all kinds of consequences; it doesn't matter. But to see the totality of this misery, you need great freedom to look; and that very looking is the disciplining of the mind, it brings its own discipline. Out of that freedom there comes silence, and you'll have answered your question.

## — 4 —
## *Religions and Nations Cause War*

So, what brings disorder in the world, psychologically, inwardly? Obviously, one of the reasons for this enormous, destructive disorder in the world is the division of religions—you a Hindu and I a Muslim; you a Christian: Catholic, Protestant, Episcopalian—a multitude of divisions... So, religions have separated man, and that is one of the factors of great disorder. You are not agreeing with me, you see the facts... And nationalism, a recent poisonous growth, is also the cause of disorder.... And as long as you have sovereign governments—that is, nationalistic, separate governments, sovereign governments with their armies—you are bound to have wars.

## — 5 —
## *Can We Earn a Living without Hurting Others?*

What do we mean by livelihood? It is the earning of one's needs, food, clothing, and shelter, is it not? The difficulty of livelihood arises only when we use the essentials of life—food, clothing, and shelter—as a means of psychological aggression. That is, when I use the needs, the necessities, as a means of self-aggrandizement, then the problem of livelihood arises; and our society is essentially based, not on supplying the essentials, but on psychological aggrandizement using the essentials as psychological expansion of oneself.

## — 6 —
## *What Is a Wrong Profession?*

Surely we can see what is a wrong profession. To be a soldier, a policeman, a lawyer, is obviously a wrong profession because they thrive on conflict, on dissension; and the big businessman, the capitalist, thrives on exploitation. The big businessman may be an individual, or it may be the state—if the state takes over big business it does not cease to exploit you and me. And as society is based on the army, the police, the law, the big businessman—that is, on the principle of dissension, exploitation, and violence—how can you and I, who want a decent, right profession, survive? There is increasing unemployment, greater armies; larger police forces with their secret service; and big business is becoming bigger and bigger, forming vast corporations, which are eventually taken over by the state, for the state has become a great corporation in certain countries. Given this situation of exploitation, of a society built on dissension, how are you going to find a right livelihood? Most of us are concerned with getting a job and sticking to it in the hope of advancement with more and more pay. Because each one of us wants safety, security, a permanent position, there is no radical revolution. It is not those who are self-satisfied, contented, but only the adventurous, those who want to experiment with their lives, with their existence, who discover the real things, a new way of living.

So, before there can be a right livelihood, the obviously false means of earning a livelihood must first be seen—the army, the law, the police, the big business corporations that are sucking people in and exploiting them, whether in the name of the state, of capital, or of religion. When you see the false and eradicate the false, there is transformation, there is revolution; and it is that revolution alone that can create a new society. To seek, as an individual, a right livelihood is good, is excellent, but that does not solve the vast problem.

The vast problem is solved only when you and I are not seeking security. There is no such thing as security. When you seek security, what happens? What is happening in the world at the present time? All Europe wants security, is crying for it, and what is happening? They want security through their nationalism. After all, you are a nationalist because you want security, and you think that through nationalism you are going to have security. It has been proved over and over again that you cannot have security through nationalism because nationalism is a process of isolation, inviting wars, misery, and destruction. So, right livelihood on a vast scale must begin with those who understand what is false. When you are battling against the false, then you are creating the right means of livelihood. When you are battling against the whole structure of dissension, of exploitation, whether by the left or by the right, or the authority of religion and the priests, that is the right profession at the present time because that will create a new society, a new culture. But to battle, you must see very clearly and very definitely that which is false so that the false drops away. To discover what is false, you must be aware of it; you must observe everything that you are doing, thinking, and feeling, and out of that you will not only discover what is false, but out of that there will come a new vitality, a new energy, and that energy will dictate what kind of work to do or not to do.

## — 7 —
## *You Have to Be a Law to Yourself*

But after all, truth is something that cannot be given to you. You have to find it out for yourself. And to find it out for yourself, you must be a law to yourself, you must be a guide to yourself, not the political man that is going to save the world, not the communist, not the leader, not the priest, not the sannyasi, not the books; you have to live, you have to be a law to yourself. And therefore no authority—which means completely standing alone, not outwardly, but inwardly completely alone, which means no fear.

## — 8 —
## *Responsibility Belongs to Each One of Us*

And that peace is your responsibility, the responsibility of each one of us, not the politician, not the soldier, not the lawyer, not the businessman, not the communist, socialist, nobody. It is your responsibility, how you live, how you live your daily life. If you want peace in the world, you have to live peacefully, not hating each other, not being envious, not seeking power, not pursuing competition. Because out of that freedom from these, you have love. It is only a mind that is capable of loving that will know what it is to live peacefully.

CHAPTER TWELVE

# RACE, CULTURE, COUNTRY

## — 1 —

## *There Is Only One Human Race: What Is Your Relationship to It?*

If one may point out, this division of people as of the West or of the East is geographic and arbitrary, is it not? It has no fundamental significance. Whether we live east or west of a certain line, whether we are brown, black or white, we are all human beings, suffering and hoping, fearful and believing; joy and pain exist here as they exist there. Thought is not of the West or of the East, but man divides it according to his conditioning. Love is not geographic, held as sacred on one continent and denied on another. The division of human beings is for economic and exploiting purposes. This does not mean that individuals are not different in temperament, and so on; there is similarity, and yet there is difference. All this is fairly obvious and psychologically factual, is it not?

## — 2 —
## *Civilizations May Vary: Fundamentals of the Human Condition Are the Same*

Seeing the difference, we must yet be aware of the similarity. The outward expressions may and do vary, but behind these outward forms and manifestations the urges, compulsions, longings, and fears are similar. Do not let us be deceived by words. Both here and there, man wants to have peace and plenty, and to find something more than material happiness. Civilizations may vary according to climate, environment, food, and so on, but culture throughout the world is fundamentally the same: to be compassionate, to shun evil, to be generous, not to be envious, to forgive, and so on. Without this fundamental culture, any civilization, whether here or there, will disintegrate or be destroyed. Knowledge may be acquired by the so-called backward peoples, they can very soon learn the 'know-how' of the West; they too can be warmongers, generals, lawyers, policemen, and tyrants. But culture is an entirely different matter.

The love of God and the freedom of man are not so easily come by, and without these, material welfare doesn't mean much.

## — 3 —
## *Division Is False Security*

In our urge to be secure, not only as individuals, but as groups, nations, and races, have we not built a world in which war, within and outside of a particular society, has become the major concern?...

Peace is a state of mind; it is the freedom from all desire

to be secure. The mind-heart that seeks security must always be in the shadow of fear. Our desire is not only for material security, but much more for inner, psychological security, and it is this desire to be inwardly secure through virtue, through belief, through a nation, that creates limiting and so conflicting groups and ideas.

## — 4 —
## *If You Change, It Changes the World*

How extraordinarily important it is that there should be at least some who do not belong to any particular group or race or to any specialized religion or society. They will create the true brotherhood of man for they will be seeking the truth.

To be free from outward riches there must be the awareness of inward poverty, which brings untold riches. The stream of culture may change its course through a few awakened people. These are not strangers but you and me.

A stone may direct the course of a river; so a small number may direct the course of a culture. Surely any great thing is done in this manner.

## — 5 —
## *Legislation Does Not Put an End to Crime*

Periodically one group exploits another group, and the exploitation brings on a violent crisis. This has been happening throughout the ages—one race dominating, exploiting, murdering another race and in turn being oppressed, cheated, poverty-stricken. How is this to be solved? Is it to be adjusted only through outward legislation, outward organization, outward education, or by understanding the inner conflicting causes that have produced the outer chaos and misery? You cannot grasp the inner without understanding the outer. If you merely try to put down one race exploiting or oppressing another, then you will become the exploiter, the oppressor. If you adopt evil methods for a righteous end, the end is transformed by the means. So until we grasp this deeply, lastingly, mere reformation of evil by evil methods is productive of further evil; thus reform ever needs further reform. We think we see its obviousness, and yet we allow ourselves to be persuaded to the contrary through fear, propaganda, and so on, which means really that we do not grasp its truth.

## — 6 —
## *Free Yourself from Bondage, and You Free the World*

As the individual, so the nation, so the state; you may not be able to transform another, but you can be certain of your own transformation. You may stop one country exploiting another by violent methods, by economic sanctions, and so on, but what guarantee is here that the very nation that is putting an end to the ruthlessness of another is not going to be also oppressive, ruthless? There is no guarantee, no guarantee whatsoever. On the contrary, in fighting evil by evil means, the nation, the individual becomes that which he is fighting.

You may build an outer, superficial structure of excellent legislation to control, to check, but if there is no goodwill and brotherly love, the inward conflict and poverty explode and produce chaos. Mere legislation does not prevent the West from exploiting the East or perhaps the East from exploiting the West in its turn, but just as long as we, individually or in groups, identify ourselves with this or that race, nation, or religion, so long will there be wars and exploitation, oppression, and starvation. Just as long as you admit to yourself division, the long list of absurd divisions as an American, Englishman, German, Hindu, and so on, just as long as you are not aware of human unity and relationship, so long will there be mass murder and sorrow. A people that is guided, checked by mere legislation is as an artificial flower, beautiful to look upon but empty within.

You will probably say that the world will not wait for individual awakening or for the awakening of a few to alter its course. Yes, it will go on its blind, set course. But it will awaken through each individual who can throw off his bondage to division, to worldliness, to personal ambition and power; through his understanding, through his compassion can brutality and ignorance be brought to an end. In his awakening only is there hope.

## CHAPTER THIRTEEN

# YOU AND THE WORLD

### — 1 —

### *What Is Your Relationship to the World?*

So, what is the relationship between ourselves and the world? Is the world different from us, or is each one of us the result of a total process, not separate from the world, but part of the world? That is, you and I are the result of a world process, of a total process, not of a separate, individualistic process because, after all, you are the result of the past, you are conditioned through environmental influences—political, social, economic, geographical, climatic, and so on. You are the result of the total process; therefore, you are not separate from the world.

### — 2 —

### *You Are the World: What You Are, the World Is*

You are the world, and what you are the world is. Therefore the world's problem is your problem, and if you solve your problem, you solve the world's problem. So, the world is not separate from the individual. To try to solve the world's problem without solving your individual problem is futile, utterly empty, because you and I make up the world.... Because, after all, the world is not distant from you; it is where you live, the world of your family, of your friends, of your neighbors; and if you and I can fundamentally transform ourselves, then there is a possibility of changing the world, and not otherwise.

## — 3 —
## *All Great Changes in the World Have Begun with a Few, with You and with Me*

That is why all great changes and reforms in the world have begun with a few, with individuals, with you and me. So-called mass action is merely the collective action of individuals who are convinced, and mass action has significance only when the individuals in the mass are awake; but if they are hypnotized by words, by an ideology, then mass action must lead to disaster.

So, seeing that the world is in an appalling mess, with impending wars, starvation, the disease of nationalism, with corrupt organized religious ideologies at work—recognizing all this, it is obvious that to bring about a fundamental, radical revolution, we must begin with ourselves. You may say, "I am willing to change myself, but it will take an infinite number of years if each individual is to change." But is that a fact? Let it take a number of years. If you and I are really convinced, really see the truth that revolution must begin with ourselves and not with somebody else, will it take very long to convince, to transform the world? Because you are the world, your actions will affect the world you live in, which is the world of your relationships. But the difficulty is to recognize the importance of individual transformation. We demand world transformation, the transformation of society about us, but we are blind, unwilling to transform ourselves. What is society?

Surely, it is the relationship between you and me. What you are and what I am produces relationship and creates society, whether it calls itself Hindu, communist, capitalist, or what you will, our relationship has to change, and relationship does not depend on legislation, on governments, on outward circumstances, but entirely upon you and me.

## — 4 —
## *Helping and Serving Other People*

*Questioner*: I want to help people, serve them. What is the best way?

*Krishnamurti*: The best way is to begin to understand yourself and change yourself. In this desire to help another, to serve another, there is hidden pride, conceit. If you love, you serve. The clamor to help is born of vanity. If you want to help another, you must know yourself for you are the other. Outwardly we may be different but we are all driven by craving, by fear, by greed, or by ambition; inwardly we are very much alike. Without self-knowledge, how can you have knowledge of another's needs? Without understanding yourself, you cannot understand another, serve another. Without self-knowledge you are acting in ignorance, and so creating sorrow.

Let us consider this. Industrialization is spreading rapidly throughout the world, urged on by greed and war. Industrialization may give employment, feed more people, but what is the larger result? What happens to a people highly developed in technique? They will be richer, there will be more cars, more airplanes, more gadgets, more cinema shows, bigger and better houses; but what happens to them as human beings? They become more and more ruthless, more and more mechanical, less and less creative. Violence must spread and government then is the organization of violence. Industrialization may bring about better economic conditions, but with what appalling results—slums, antagonism of the worker against the non-worker, the boss and the slave, capitalism and communism, the whole chaotic business that is spreading in different parts of the world. Happily we say that it will raise the standard of living, poverty will be stamped out, there will be work, there will be freedom, dignity, and so on.

The division of the rich and the poor, the man of power and the seeker after power—this endless division and conflict will go on. What is the end of it? What has happened in the West? Wars, revolutions, continual threat of destruction, utter despair. Who is bringing help to whom and who is serving whom? When everything is being destroyed about you, the thoughtful must inquire as to the deeper causes, which so few seem to do.

## — 5 —
## *The Causes of War Are in You, Not Technology*

You cannot destroy industry, you cannot do away with the airplane, but you can eradicate utterly the causes that produce its misuse. The causes of its appalling use lie in you. You can eradicate them, which is a difficult task; since you will not face that task, you try to legalize war; you have covenants, leagues, international security, and so on, but greed, ambition overrule them and war and catastrophe inevitably follow.

## — 6 —
## *The Self Is a Book of Many Volumes*

To help another, you must know yourself; like you, he is the result of the past. We are all interrelated. If you are inwardly diseased by ignorance, ill will, and passion, you will inevitably spread disease and darkness. If you are inwardly healthy and integrated, you spread light and peace; otherwise you help to produce greater chaos, greater misery. To understand oneself requires patience, tolerant awareness; the self is a book of many volumes which you cannot read in a day, but when once you begin to read, you must read every word, every sentence, every paragraph, for in them are the intimations of the whole. The beginning of it is the ending of it. If you know how to read, supreme wisdom is to be found.

## — 7 —
## *Can Human Beings Change?*

Seeing all this, as you must, one demands naturally: Can human beings change? Can you and I change? Can you and I bring about in ourselves a mutation so profound that, as human beings, our relationship is not based on temporary, convenient, self-centered activity? Because what is most important is relationship. Unless there is a radical revolution in that relationship between two human beings, talking about God or about the scriptures, or going back to the Vedas, the Bible, and the rest of it, is sheer nonsense. It has no meaning whatsoever unless we establish right relationship between human beings.

## — 8 —
## *Right Relationship between Human Beings*

And that will be the subject of our talk—how to bring about a fundamental revolution in our relationship so that there will be no war, so that countries are not divided by nationalities, by frontiers, by class differences, and so on. Unless we, you and I, establish such a relationship, not theoretically, not ideologically, not hypothetically, but actually, factually, there is bound to be a greater and greater decline and deterioration.

What do we mean by relationship? What does it mean to be related? First of all, are we related? Relationship means contact: to be together, to be related, to be in contact, to be in immediate contact with another human being, to know all his difficulties, his problems, his misery, his anxiety, which is your own. And in understanding yourself you understand the human being and, therefore, bring about a radical transformation in society. The "individual" has very little meaning, but the "human being" has a tremendous significance. The individual may change according to pressures, strains, circumstances; but his change will not radically affect society. But the problems of man, not as an individual but as a human being who has lived for two million years and much more, with his conflicts, with his anxieties, with his fears, with his coming face to face with death—the whole of that is the human issue. Unless we understand that—not as an individual, but as a human being—there is no possibility of bringing about a different culture, a different society.

## — 9 —
## *Relationship Is Not between Images*

Are we related? Is one human being related to another? We mean by relationship, don't we, to be in contact intellectually, emotionally, psychologically. Are we in such contact? Or, is there contact, relationship, between the image that you have about yourself and the image you have about another? You have an image about yourself, ideas about yourself, concepts, experiences, and so on. You have your particular idiosyncrasies, tendencies—all that has built an image about yourself...

You have an image carved by the mind, or carved through your experience, through tradition, through circumstances, through strange pressures. There is that image of yourself, and the other person also has an image of himself. So these two images come into contact, and that is what we call relationship. Whether it is the most intimate relationship between a husband and wife or the image you have created about Russia, about America, about Vietnam, about this or that, the contact between the two images is what we call relationship. Please do follow this. That is all the relationship we know. You have an image about yourself, and you have created an image about another—whether he is an American or a Russian or a Chinese or this or that. You have an image about the Pakistani; you have an image about the Hindu, the Indian, with a line called the frontier—and you are willing to kill each other for the sake of that image, and that image is strengthened through a flag, through national spirit, through hatred, and so on. So you are willing—please listen—to kill each other for the sake of a word, of an idea, of an image....

Man has not solved the problem of war. The first woman

or the father must have cried out at the first battle. We are still crying.

## — 10 —
## *To Establish Right Relationship, We Must Destroy the Image*

So to establish right relationship is to destroy the image. Do you understand what it means to destroy the image? It means to destroy the image about yourself—that you are a Hindu, that I am a Pakistani, a Muslim, a Catholic, a Jew, or a communist, and so on. You have to destroy the machinery that creates the image—the machinery that is in you and the machinery that is in the other. Otherwise you may destroy one image, and the machinery will create another image. So one has not only to find out the existence of the image—that is, to be aware of your particular image—but also to be aware of what the machinery is that creates the image.

## — 11 —
## *The Image Is Put Together by Thought Which Is the Response of Memory*

Perhaps you have understood the word, how it is created by knowledge, by experience, by tradition, by the various strains and stresses in family life, work in the office, the insults—all that makes up the image. What is the machinery that makes that image? You understand? The image must be put together.

The image must be maintained; otherwise, it will collapse. So you must find out for yourself how this machinery works.

And when you understand the nature of the machinery and the significance of that machinery, then the image itself ceases to be—the image—not only the conscious image, the image that you have of yourself consciously and are aware of superficially, but also the image deep down, the whole of it. I hope I am making this thing clear.

One has to go into it and find out how the image comes into being and if it is possible to stop the machinery that creates it. Then only is there a relationship between human beings—it will not be between two images, which are dead entities. It is very simple.

## — 12 —
## *The Thinker, the 'Me', Is the Image-Maker*

You flatter me, you respect me; and I have an image about you, through insult, through flattery. I have experience—pain, death, misery, conflict, hunger, loneliness. All that creates an image in me; I am that image. Not that I am the image, not that the image and I are different; but the 'me' is that image; the thinker is that image. It is the thinker that creates the image. Through his responses, through his reactions—physical, psychological, intellectual, and so on—the thinker, the observer, the experiencer, creates that image through memory, through thought. So the machinery is thinking, the machinery comes into existence through thought. And thought is necessary; otherwise, you cannot exist.

## — 13 —
## *Thinking Has Its Proper Place in Daily Life*

So, first see the problem. Thought creates the thinker. The thinker begins to create the image about himself: he is the Atman, he is God, he is the soul, he is a Brahmin, he is a non-Brahmin, he is a Muslim, he is a Hindu, and the rest of it. He creates the image and he lives in it. So thinking is the beginning of this machinery. And you will say, "How can I stop thinking?" You cannot. But one can think and not create the image.

## — 14 —
## *Opinions of Each Other Are Not Relationship*

So one begins to see that most of our relationship is actually based on this image-formation, and having formed the image, one establishes or hopes to establish relationship between two images. And naturally there is no relationship between images. If you have an opinion about me and if I have an opinion about you, how can we have any relationship? Relationship exists only when it is free, when there is freedom from this image-formation—we will go into this during the talks that come. Only when this image is broken up and the image-formation ceases will there be the ending of conflict, the total ending of conflict. Then only will there be peace, not only inwardly, but also outwardly. It is only when you have established that peace inwardly that the mind, being free, can go very far.

You know, freedom can only exist when the mind is not in conflict. Most of us are in conflict, unless we are dead. You hypnotize yourself, or identify yourself with some cause, some commitment, some philosophy, some sect, or some belief—you are so identified that you are just mesmerized, and you live in a state of sleep. Most of us are in conflict; the ending of that conflict is freedom. With conflict you cannot have freedom. You may seek, you may want it; but you can never have it.

So relationship means the ending of the machinery which puts together the image, and with the ending of that machinery, right relationship is established. Therefore there is the ending of conflict.

SECTION THREE

# WHAT IS THE PURPOSE OF LIFE?

CHAPTER FOURTEEN

# WHAT IS LIFE?

## — 1 —
## *What Is the Purpose of Life?*

So, in discussing what is the purpose of life, we have to find out what we mean by and what we mean by—not merely the dictionary meaning, but the significance we give to those words. Surely, life implies everyday action, everyday thought, everyday feeling, does it not? It implies the struggles, the pains, the anxieties, the deceptions, the worries, the routine of the office, of business, of bureaucracy, and so on. All that is life, is it not? By life we mean, not just one department or one layer of consciousness, but the total process of existence which is our relationship to things, to people, to ideas. That is what we mean by life—not an abstract thing.

So, if that is what we mean by life, then has life a purpose? Or is it because we do not understand the ways of life—the everyday pain, anxiety, fear, ambition, greed—because we do not understand the daily activities of existence that we want a purpose, remote or near, far away or close?

— 2 —

## *Why Do We Want a Purpose?*

We want a purpose so that we can guide our everyday life towards an end. That is obviously what we mean by purpose. But if I understand how to live, then the very living is in itself sufficient, is it not? Do we then want a purpose? If I love you, if I love another, is that not sufficient in itself? Do I then want a purpose? Surely, we want a purpose only when we do not understand or when we want a mode of conduct with an end in view. After all, most of us are seeking a way of life, a way of conduct, and we either look to others, to the past, or we try to find a mode of behavior through our own experience. When we look to our own experience for a pattern of behavior, our experience is always conditioned, is it not? However wide the experiences one may have had, unless these experiences dissolve the past conditioning, any new experiences only further strengthen the past conditioning.

That is a fact which we can discuss. And if we look to another, to the past, to a guru, to an ideal, to an example for a pattern of behavior, we are merely forcing the extraordinary vitality of life into a mold, into a particular shape, and thereby we lose the swiftness, the intensity, the richness of life.

— 3 —

## *To Find Out the Purpose of Life, the Mind Must Be Free of Measurement*

So, we must find out very clearly what we mean by purpose, if there is a purpose. You may say there is a purpose: to reach reality, God, or what you will. But to reach that, you must know it, you must be aware of it, you must have the measure, the depth, the significance of it. Do we know reality for ourselves, or do we know it only through the authority of another? So, can you say that the purpose of life is to find reality when you do not know what reality is? Since reality is the unknown, the mind that seeks the unknown must first be free from the known, must it not? If my mind is clouded, burdened with the known, it can only measure according to its own condition, its own limitation, and therefore it can never know the unknown, can it?

So, what we are trying to discuss and find out is whether life has a purpose, and whether that purpose can be measured.

It can only be measured in terms of the known, in terms of the past; and when I measure the purpose of life in terms of the known, I will measure it according to my likes and dislikes. Therefore, the purpose will be conditioned by my desires, and therefore it ceases to be the purpose. Surely, that is clear, is it not? I can understand what is the purpose of life only through the screen of my own prejudices, wants, and desires—otherwise I cannot judge, can I? So, the measure, the tape, the yardstick, is a conditioning of my mind, and according to the dictates of my conditioning. I will decide what the purpose is. But is that the purpose of life? It is created by my want, and therefore it is surely not the purpose of life. To find out the purpose of life, the mind must be free of measurement, then only can it find out—otherwise, you are merely projecting your own want. This is not mere intellection, and if you go into it deeply, you will see its significance.

— 4 —

## *It Is Only in Freedom that One Can Discover Any Truth*

After all, it is according to my prejudice, to my want, to my desire, to my predilection, that I decide what the purpose of life is to be. So, my desire creates the purpose. Surely, that is not the purpose of life. Which is more important—to find out the purpose of life, or to free the mind itself from its own conditioning and then inquire? And perhaps when the mind is free from its own conditioning, that very freedom itself is the purpose. Because, after all, it is only in freedom that one can discover any truth.

So, the first requisite is freedom, and not seeking the purpose of life. Without freedom, obviously, one cannot find it; without being liberated from our own petty little wants, pursuits, ambitions, envies, and ill will—without freedom from these things, how can one possibly inquire or discover what is the purpose of life?

— 5 —

## *Do We Want to Understand Interrelationship, or Only to Escape Pain?*

So, is it not important, for one who is inquiring about the purpose of life, to find out first if the instrument of inquiry is capable of penetrating into the processes of life, into the psychological complexities of one's own being? Because, that is all we have, is it not?—a psychological instrument that is shaped to suit our own needs. And as the instrument is fashioned out of our own petty desires, as it is the outcome of our own experiences, worries, anxieties, and ill will, now can such an instrument find reality? Therefore, is it not important, if you are to inquire into the purpose of life, to find out first if the inquirer is capable of understanding or discovering what the purpose is? I am not turning the tables on you, but that is what is implied when we inquire about the purpose of life. When we ask that question, we have first to find out whether the questioner, the inquirer, is capable of understanding. Now, when we discuss the purpose of life, we see that we mean by life the extraordinarily complex state of interrelationship without which there would be no life. And if we do not understand the full significance of that life, its varieties, its impressions, and so on, what is the good of inquiring about the purpose of life? If I do not understand my relationship with you, my relationship with property and ideas, how can I go further? After all, to find truth or God, or what you will, I must first understand my existence, I must understand the life around me and in me; otherwise, the search for reality becomes merely an escape from everyday action, and as most of us do not understand everyday action, as for most of us life is drudgery, pain, suffering, anxiety, we say, "For God's sake, tell us how to escape from it." That is what most of us want—a drug to put us to sleep so that we don't feel the aches and pains of life.

## — 6 —
## *Do We Want to Understand Life or Escape It?*

Deeply our life is a confusion, a mess, a misery, an agony. The more sensitive we are, the more the despair, the anxiety, the guilt feeling, and naturally we want to escape from it because we haven't found an answer; we don't know how to get out of this confusion. We want to go to some other realm, to another dimension. We escape through music, through art, through literature, but it is just an escape; it has no reality in comparison with what we are seeking. All escapes are similar, whether through the door of a church, through God or a savior, through the door of drink or of various drugs.

We must not only understand what and why we are seeking, but we must also understand this demand for deep, abiding experience, because it is only the mind that does not seek at all, that does not demand any experience in any form, that can enter into a realm, into a dimension that is totally new.

That is what we are going into this evening, I hope. Our lives are shallow, insufficient in themselves, and we want something else, a greater, deeper experience. Also, we are astonishingly isolated. All our activity, all our thinking, all our behavior leads to this isolation, this loneliness, and we want to escape from it.

CHAPTER FIFTEEN

# YOUR RELATIONSHIP TO NATURE, ANIMALS, THE WHOLE EARTH

## — 1 —

## *What Is Your Relationship with Nature?*

I do not know if you have discovered your relationship with nature. There is no "right" relationship, there is only the understanding of relationship. Right relationship implies the mere acceptance of a formula, as does right thought. Right thought and right thinking are two different things. Right thought is merely conforming to what is right, what is respectable, whereas right thinking is movement, it is the product of understanding, and understanding is constantly undergoing modification, change. Similarly there is a difference between right relationship and understanding our relationship with nature. What is your relationship with nature?—nature being the rivers, the trees, the swift-flying birds, the fish in the water, the minerals under the earth, the waterfalls and shallow pools. What is your relationship to them? Most of us are not aware of that relationship.

We never look at a tree, or if we do, it is with a view of

using that tree—either to sit in its shade or to cut it down for lumber. In other words, we look at trees with a utilitarian purpose; we never look at a tree without projecting ourselves and utilizing it for our own convenience. We treat the earth and its products in the same way. There is no love of earth, there is only usage of earth. If one really loved the earth, there would be frugality in using the things of the earth. That is, if we were to understand our relationship with the earth, we should be very careful in the use we made of the things of the earth. The understanding of one's relationship with nature is as difficult as understanding one's relationship with one's neighbor, wife, and children. But we have not given a thought to it, we have never sat down to look at the stars, the moon, or the trees. We are too busy with social or political activities. Obviously these activities are escapes from ourselves, and to worship nature is also an escape from ourselves.

We are always using nature, either as an escape or for utilitarian ends—we never actually stop and love the earth or the things of the earth, never enjoy the rich fields, though we utilize them to feed and clothe ourselves. We never like to till the earth with our hands—we are ashamed to work with our hands. There is an extraordinary thing that takes place when you work the earth with your hands.

## — 2 —
## *We Have Lost Our Relationship with Nature*

So, we have lost our relationship with nature. If once we understood that relationship, its real significance, then we would not divide property into yours and mine; though one might own a piece of land and build a house on it, it would cease to be "mine" or "yours" in the exclusive sense—it would be more a means of taking shelter. Because we do not love the earth and the things of the earth but merely utilize them, we are insensitive to the beauty of a waterfall, we have lost the touch of life, we have never sat with our backs against the trunk of a tree; and since we do not love nature, we do not know how to love human beings and animals. Go down the street and watch how the bullocks are treated, their tails all out of shape. You shake your head and say, "Very sad." But we have lost the sense of tenderness, that sensitivity, that response to things of beauty; and it is only in the renewal of that sensitivity that we can have understanding of what is true relationship. That sensitivity does not come in the mere hanging of a few pictures, or in painting a tree, or putting a few flowers in your hair; sensitivity comes only when this utilitarian outlook is put aside. It does not mean that you cannot use the earth, but you must use the earth as it is to be used.

## — 3 —
## *It Is Our World—Not Yours or Mine*

This is our world, is it not? It is our earth, not the businessman's earth or the poor man's earth. It is our earth. It is not a communist world nor the capitalist world, it is our world in which to live, to enjoy, to be happy. That is the first necessity, to have that feeling—which is not a sentiment but an actuality in which there is love, a feeling that it is "ours." Without that feeling, mere legislation or union wages or working for the state—which is another kind of boss—is of very little meaning; then we become merely employees either of the state or of a businessman. But when there is the feeling that this is "our earth," then there will be no employer and the employed, no feeling that the one is the boss and the other is the employee, but we have not that feeling of 'ourness'; each man is out for himself; each nation, each group, each party, each religion is out for itself. We are human beings living on this earth; it is our earth to be cherished, to be created, to be cared for. Without that feeling, we want to create a new world. So every kind of experiment is being made—sharing profits, compulsory work, union wages, legislation, compulsion—every form of coercion, persuasion, is used...

There are so many ways. But without this extraordinary feeling that we are one humanity, that this is our earth, mere legislation and compulsion or persuasion will only lead to further destruction and further misery.

## — 4 —

## *To Provide Food, Clothing, Shelter for All Requires Psychological, not Political, Revolution*

To bring about an equitable distribution of food, clothing, and shelter, a totally different kind of social organization is necessary, is it not? Separate nationalities and their sovereign governments, power blocks and conflicting economic structures, as well as the caste system and organized religions—each of these proclaims its way to be the only true way. All these must cease to be, which means that the whole hierarchical, authoritarian attitude towards life must come to an end... It is a complete psychological revolution, and such a revolution is essential if man throughout the world is not to be in want of the basic physical necessities. The earth is ours, it is not English, Russian, or American, nor does it belong to any ideological group. We are human beings, not Hindus, Buddhists, Christians, or Muslims.

## — 5 —
## *Love, the Beauty of the Earth, Answers Any Problem*

Watch yourselves; watch the leaf there. Watch the beauty of the sunset, the beauty of the earth, the hill, the curve of a hill, the flowing water; watch the beauty of a fine, refined mind, the good mind, the beauty of a face, the beauty of a smile. You have denied all that because you have associated beauty with pleasure, and pleasure with sex and so-called love. Beauty is not that at all. Beauty is not something merely related to pleasure. To understand beauty one must have an extraordinarily simple mind—that is, a mind unclouded by thought, that can look at things as they are, that can see the sunset with all the color, loveliness, and light, that can look at it simply, without verbalization, and be in contact, in communion with it without the word, without the gesture, without the memory, so that there is not "you" and the object which "you" are looking at. That extraordinary communion without the object, without the thinker and the thought and the object and experience, that sense of immense space—that is beauty. And that is also love. Without love, do what you will—you may do social work, social reforms, parliamentary government, you may marry, have children—you will find no answer to any problem in life. With love you can do what you will. With love there is virtue and there is humility.

## — 6 —
## *Killing Animals*

The problem is that of killing, and not merely killing animals for food. A man is not virtuous because he doesn't eat meat, nor is he any less virtuous because he does. The god of a petty mind is also petty; his pettiness is measured by that of the mind which puts flowers at his feet. The larger issue includes the many and apparently separate problems that man has created within himself and outside of himself. Killing is really a very great and complex problem. Shall we consider it? There are many forms of killing, are there not? There is killing by a word or a gesture, killing in fear or in anger, killing for a country or an ideology, killing for a set of economic dogmas or religious beliefs...

With a word or a gesture you may kill a man's reputation; through gossip, defamation, contempt, you may wipe him out. And does not comparison kill? Don't you kill a boy by comparing him with another who is cleverer or more skillful? A man who kills out of hate or anger is regarded as a criminal and put to death. Yet the man who deliberately bombs thousands of people off the face of the earth in the name of his country is honored, decorated; looked upon as a hero. Killing is spreading over the earth. For the safety or expansion of one nation, another is destroyed. Animals are killed for food, for profit, or for so-called sport; they are vivisected for the "well-being" of man. The soldier exists to kill. Extraordinary progress is being made in the technology of murdering vast numbers of people in a few seconds and at great distances. Many scientists are wholly occupied with it, and priests bless the bomber and the warship. Also, we kill a cabbage or a carrot in order to eat; we destroy a pest. Where are we to draw the line beyond which we will not kill?... So the issue we are discussing is not merely the killing or the non-killing of animals, but the cruelty and hate that are ever increasing in the world and in each one of us. That is our real problem, isn't it?

## — 7 —
## *Be Part of the Wholeness*

That afternoon the sun was on the meadow, and on the tall, dark trees that stood around it, carved in green, stately, without movement. With your preoccupations and inward chatter, with your mind and eyes all over the place, restlessly wondering if the rain would catch you on your way back, you felt as though you were trespassing, not wanted there; but soon you were part of it, part of that enchanted solitude.

There were no birds of any kind; the air was completely still, and the tops of the trees were motionless against the blue sky. The lush green meadow was the center of this world, and as you sat on a rock, you were part of that center. It wasn't imagination; imagination is silly. It wasn't that you were trying to identify yourself with what was so splendidly open and beautiful; identification is vanity. It wasn't that you were trying to forget or abnegate yourself in this unspoiled solitude of nature; all self-forgetful abnegation is arrogance.

It wasn't the shock or the compulsion of so much purity; all compulsion is a denial of the true. You could do nothing to make yourself, or help yourself to be, part of that wholeness. But you were part of it, part of the green meadow, the hard rock, the blue sky and the stately trees. It was so. You might remember it, but then you would not be of it; and if you went back to it, you would never find it.

CHAPTER SIXTEEN

# GOD, THE UNIVERSE, THE UNKNOWN

— 1 —

## *What Is a Religious Mind?*

The religious mind isn't the mind that believes, that goes to church every day, or once a week; it isn't the mind that has a creed, that is bound by dogmas and superstitions. The religious mind is really a scientific mind—scientific in the sense that it is able to observe facts without distortion, to see itself as it is. To be free of one's conditioning requires, not a believing or accepting mind, but a mind that is capable of observing itself rationally, sanely, and seeing the fact that unless there is a total breaking up of the psychological structure of society—which is the 'me'—there can be no innocency, and that without innocency, the mind can never be religious.

— 2 —

## *Words and Beliefs Are Not God*

The religious mind is not fragmentary; it does not divide life into compartments. It comprehends the totality of life—the life of sorrow and pain, the life of joy and passing satisfactions. Being totally free from the psychological structure of ambition, greed, envy, competition, from all demand for the 'more', the religious mind is in a state of innocency; and it is only such a mind that can go beyond itself, not the mind that merely believes in a beyond, or that has some hypothesis about God.

The word is not God; the concept you have of God is not God. To find out if there is that which may be called God, all verbal concepts and formulations, all ideas, all thought, which is the response of memory, must come totally to an end. Only then is there that state of innocency in which there is no self-deception, no wanting, no desire for a result; and then you will find out for yourself what is true...

You cannot hold the waters of the sea in a garment or capture the wind in your fist. But you can listen to the deep murmurings of the storm, to the violence of the sea; you can feel the enormous power of the wind, its beauty and its destructiveness. For you must destroy totally the old for something new to be.

## — 3 —
## *Freedom from the Known*

You cannot possibly talk about the unknown. No word, no concept can ever bring it within the framework of the known.

The word is not the thing, and the thing must be seen directly without the word. And that is extraordinarily difficult: to see something out of innocency. To see something out of love—love which has never been contaminated by jealousy, by hate, by anger, by attachment, by possession. One must die to attachment, to possession, to jealousy, to envy—die without reason, without cause, without motive. And it is only then, in this freedom from the known, that the other thing may be.

## — 4 —
## *Meditation Is Not Mantra, Prayer, Ritual, or Other Form of Drug*

Meditation cannot come about through any repetition of words, through what the Hindus call mantras and you call prayer. Prayers and mantras only put the mind to sleep. By droning a series of words over and over again, you can put yourself to sleep very nicely—which is what many of us do.

In that soporific condition we feel we have achieved a most extraordinary state, but that is not meditation. That is merely drugging yourself with words. You can also drug yourself by taking certain chemicals, or by drinking, and in various other ways; but that is obviously not meditation.

Meditation is really extraordinary, and it is something you must do every day. But meditation is not separate from living.

It is not something to be done in the morning and forgotten for the rest of the day—or remembered and used as a guide in your life. That is not meditation.

Meditation is an awareness of every thought, of every feeling, of every act, and that awareness can come into being only when there is no condemnation, no judgment, no comparison.

You just see everything as it is, which means that you are aware of your own conditioning, conscious as well as unconscious....

Meditation is something far beyond all this immature thinking. Meditation is that state of awareness in which there is attention to every thought and every feeling; and out of that attention there is silence—which is not the silence of discipline, control. Silence that is brought about through discipline, through control, is the silence of decay, of death. But there is a silence that comes into being naturally, effortlessly, without your even being conscious of it, when there is this attention in which there is no experiencer, no observer, no thinker. That silence is really innocency, and in that silence—without being invited, without your seeking or asking—the unknown may come.

## — 5 —
## *Life Has No Answer*

Life has no answer. Life has only one thing, one problem—which is, living. The man who lives totally, completely, every minute without choice, neither accepting nor rejecting the thing as it is, such a man is not seeking an answer, he is not asking what the purpose of life is, nor is he seeking a way out of life. But that requires great insight into oneself. Without self-knowledge, merely to seek an answer has no meaning at all because the answer will be what is most satisfactory, what is gratifying. That is what most of us want; we want to be gratified, we want to find a safe place, a heaven where there will be no disturbance. But as long as we seek, life will be disturbed.

## — 6 —
## *You Cannot Come to Truth as a Beggar*

When you pray, obviously it is an act of will; you want, you beg, you ask; as a result of your confusion, misery, suffering, you ask someone to give you knowledge, comfort, and you do have comfort. The asker generally receives what he asks for, but what he receives may not be the truth, and generally it is not the truth. You cannot come to truth as a beggar. Truth must come to you; then only you see the truth, not by asking.

But we are beggars, we everlastingly seek comfort, we seek some kind of state in which we will never be disturbed....

## — 7 —
## *To Think about the Higher Self Is Not Meditation*

To think about the higher self is not meditation. Meditation is to be aware of the activities of the mind—the mind as the meditator, how the mind divides itself as the meditator and the meditation, how the mind divides itself as the thinker and the thought, the thinker dominating thought, controlling thought, shaping thought. So in all of us, there is the thinker separate from the thought; the thinker has become the higher self, the nobler self, the Atman, or what you will, but it is still the mind divided as the thinker and the thought. The mind, seeing thought in flux, impermanent, creates the thinker as the permanent, as the Atman, which is permanent, absolute, and endless.

## — 8 —
## *The Silent, Empty Mind*

So, the cultivation of the mind or the building up of virtue is not important; that is not the emptying of the mind necessary to receive that which is eternal. The mind must be empty to receive that.

That which is measureless can only come into being, you cannot invite it, it will only come into being when the mind no longer demands, is no longer praying, asking, begging, when the mind is free, free from thought. The ending of thought is the way of meditation. There must be freedom from the known for the unknown to be. This is meditation, and this cannot come through any trick, through any practice. Practice, discipline, suppression, denial, sacrifice only strengthen the experiencer, they give him power to control himself, but that power destroys. So it is only when the mind has neither the experiencer nor the experience that there is that bliss which is, which cannot be sought, which comes into being when the mind is silent and free.

### — 9 —
### *All Human Beings Are Capable of Meditation, Not Just the Few*

As human beings we are all capable of inquiry, of discovery, and this whole process is meditation. Meditation is inquiry into the very being of the meditator....Our fear is not of the unknown but of letting go of the known. It is only when the mind allows the known to fade away that there is complete freedom from the known, and only then is it possible for the new impulse to come into being.

### — 10 —
### *God Cannot Be Captured and Put in a Cage*

You want to capture God and put Him in the cage of what you know, the cage you call the temple, the book, the guru, the system, and with that you are satisfied. By doing that you think you are becoming very religious. You are not.

## — 11 —
## *Relationship to God Is Responsibility for Everyone*

A religious person does not seek God. They are concerned with the transformation of society, which is themselves. The religious person is not the one that does innumerable rituals, follows traditions, lives in a dead, past culture, explaining endlessly the Gita or the Bible, endlessly chanting, or taking Sannyasa—that is not a religious person; they are escaping from facts. The religious person is concerned totally and completely with the understanding of society, which is themselves.

They are not separate from society. Bringing about in themselves a complete, total mutation means complete cessation of greed, envy, ambition; and therefore, they are not dependent on circumstances, though they are the result of circumstance—the food they eat, the books they read, the cinemas they go to, the religious dogmas, beliefs, rituals, and all that business. They are responsible, and therefore the religious person must understand themselves, as the product of society that they themselves have created. Therefore, to find reality they must begin here, not in a temple, not in an image—whether the image is graven by the hand or by the mind. Otherwise, how can they find something totally new, a new state?

## — 12 —
## *Religion is the Feeling of Goodness*

Do you know what religion is? It is not in the chant, it is not in the performance of puja, or any other ritual, it is not in the worship of tin gods or stone images, it is not in the temples and churches, it is not in the reading of the Bible or the Gita, it is not in the repeating of a sacred name or in the following of some other superstition invented by men. None of this is religion.

Religion is the feeling of goodness, that love which is like the river, living, moving everlastingly. In that state you will find there comes a moment when there is no longer any search at all; and this ending of search is the beginning of something totally different. The search for God, for truth, the feeling of being completely good—not the cultivation of goodness, of humility, but the seeking out of something beyond the inventions and tricks of the mind, which means having a feeling for that something, living in it, being it—that is true religion. But you can do that only when you leave the pool you have dug for yourself and go out into the river of life. Then life has an astonishing way of taking care of you, because then there is no taking care on your part. Life carries you where it will because you are part of itself; then there is no problem of security, of what people say or don't say, and that is the beauty of life.

# SOURCES AND ACKNOWLEDGEMENTS

*Abbreviation of titles by J. Krishnamurti referred to in Sources*

BOL: *The Book of Life*, Harper Collins, 1995. Copyright KFA, 1995.

CL: *Commentaries on Living*, Series I, II, III, Quest Books, 1967. Copyright 1956, KFA.

CW: *The Collected Works of J. Krishnamurti*, 1933- 1967. First Published by Kendall-Hunt, 1991/1992. Copyright 1991/1992, KFA

ESL: *Education and the Significance of Life*, Harper San Francisco, 1981. Copyright 1953, KFA

FLF: *The First and Last Freedom*, Harper San Francisco, 1975. Copyright 1954, KFA.

LA: *Life Ahead*, Harper & Row, 1975. Copyright 1963, KFA.

MWM: *Mind Without Measure*, KFI Publications, 1983. Copyright 1983, KFT.

SKR: *The Second Krishnamurti Reader*, Penguin Arkana, 1991. Copyright KFT, 1970/1971.

TOTT: *Think on These Things*, HarperPerennial, 1989. Copyright 1964, KFA.

## — *Sources* —

SECTION ONE

### *Chapter One*

1. MWM, Chap. 10, p. 79
2. FLF, Chap. 14, pp. 104-5
3. CW, Vol. 17, p. 7
4. CW, Vol. 5, p. 335
5. Ibid
6. BOL, March 16
7. CW, Vol. 5, p. 231
8. Ibid
9. Ibid
10. FLF, Question 9, pp. 180-1
11. CW, Vol. 3, pp. 159-60
12. CW, Vol. 8, pp. 337-8

### *Chapter Two*

1. SKR, Chap. 1, p.74
2. CW, Vol. 17, pp. 202-3
3. FLF, Question 22, pp. 232-3
4. FLF, Question 21, pp. 227-9
5. CL, Series III, Chap. 53, p. 294
6. CW, Vol. 16, p. 215
7. CW, Vol. 10, p. 244
8. Ibid, p. 244-5
9. Ibid, p. 245
10. CW, Vol. 14, pp. 99-100

11. Ibid, p. 100
12. CW, Vol. 15, pp. 59-60
13. SKR, Chap. 18, pp. 238-40
14. ESL, Chap 7, pp. 117-18
15. FLF, Question 21, pp. 228-9

## *Chapter Three*

1. CW, Vol. 16, p. 119
2. Ibid, pp. 119-20
3. Ibid, p. 120
4. SKR, Chap. 31, pp. 296-7
5. CW, Vol. 5, p. 216
6. Ibid, pp. 217-18
7. Ojai, 2nd Q & A, May 24, 1984
8. Ojai, 2nd Public Talk, May 3, 1981
9. CW, Vol. 15, pp. 1-2
10. CW, Vol. 6, p. 80
11. CW, Vol. 7, p. 104

## *Chapter Four*

1. Europe, 5th Public Talk, April 30, 1967
2. CW, Vol. 15, p. 90
3. CW, Vol. 6, p. 57
4. CW, Vol. 4, p. 177

## *Chapter Five*

1. Bombay, Q & A Meeting, Feb. 9, 1984
2. Brockwood Park, 2nd Q & A Meeting, Sep. 2, 1982
3. Ibid

4. CW, Vol. 5, pp. 175-6
5. Previously Unpublished Material

*Chapter Six*

1. LA, Part 1, pp. 22-4
2. ESL, Chap. 5, pp. 83-4
3. Ibid, pp. 92-4
4. Ibid, pp. 94-6
5. CW, Vol. 9, p. 155

*Chapter Seven*

1. CW, Vol. 8, p. 278
2. Ibid, pp. 278-9
3. Ibid, p. 279
4. Ibid, pp. 280-1
5. Ibid, p. 281
6. ESL, Chap. 6, p. 98
7. Ibid, pp. 98-9
8. Ibid, pp. 99-100
9. Ibid, pp. 101-2
10. Ibid, pp. 103-4

*Chapter Eight*

1. CW, Vol. 9, p. 136
2. Ibid
3. Ibid, pp. 136-7
4. Ibid, p. 138
5. Ibid, pp. 138-9
6. Ibid, p. 139

7. Ibid
8. CW, Vol. 5, p. 334
9. Ibid
10. CW, Vol. 14, p. 129
11. Ibid, pp. 130-2
12. Ibid, p. 134

SECTION TWO

## *Chapter Nine*

1. CW, Vol. 15, pp. 49-50
2. FLF, Chap. 3, pp. 36-7
3. CW, Vol. 5, p. 50
4. CW, Vol. 17, pp. 175-6
5. Ibid, p. 176
6. Ibid, p. 174
7. CW, Vol. 12, p. 144
8. CW, Vol. 14, p. 131

## *Chapter Ten*

1. CW, Vol. 17, p. 100
2. CW, Vol. 7, p. 130
3. CW, Vol. 6, p. 140
4. CW, Vol. 17, p. 164, 163
5. Ibid, p. 165
6. Ibid, p. 156-8

## *Chapter Eleven*

1. CW, Vol. 17, pp. 33-4

2. Ibid, pp. 36-7
3. Ibid, p. 37
4. CW, Vol. 15, pp. 326-7
5. CW, Vol. 5, p. 62
6. Ibid, pp. 63-4
7. CW, Vol. 15, p. 322
8. Ibid, pp. 322-3

## *Chapter Twelve*

1. CL, Series II, Chap. 44, p. 185
2. Ibid, pp. 185-6
3. Ibid, p. 186
4. CW, Vol. 3, p. 217
5. Ibid, pp. 217-18
6. Ibid, p. 218

## *Chapter Thirteen*

1. CW, Vol. 5, p. 10
2. Ibid
3. Ibid, pp. 10-11
4. CW, Vol. 3, pp. 218-19
5. Ibid, p. 219
6. Ibid
7. CW, Vol. 16, p. 43
8. Ibid
9. Ibid, pp. 43-4
10. Ibid, p. 45
11. Ibid
12. Ibid, p. 46
13. Ibid

14. Ibid

SECTION THREE

*Chapter Fourteen*

1. CW, Vol. 5, pp. 19-20
2. Ibid, p. 20
3. Ibid
4. Ibid, p. 21
5. Ibid
6. CW, Vol. 16, p. 182

*Chapter Fifteen*

1. CW, Vol. 5, p. 142
2. Ibid
3. CW, Vol. 8, p. 186
4. CL, Series III, Chap. 11, p. 44
5. CW, Vol. 15, p. 26
6. CL, Series III, Chap. 32, pp. 166-7
7. CL, Series III, Chap. 34, pp. 176-7

*Chapter Sixteen*

1. CW, Vol. 13, p. 208
2. Ibid, pp. 208-9
3. Ibid, p. 210
4. Ibid, p. 210-11
5. CW, Vol. 8. p. 184
6. Ibid, p. 192
7. Ibid

8. Ibid, pp. 193-4
9. CW, Vol. 10, p. 255
10. Ibid, p. 272
11. CW, Vol. 15, pp. 90-1
12. TOTT, Chap. 17, pp. 142-3

# RESOURCES
# SCHOOLS AND FOUNDATIONS

*— The Krishnamurti Schools —*

**UK**

**Brockwood Park School**
Bramdean, Hampshire, S024 OLQ
www.brockwood.org.uk

**USA**

**Oak Grove School**
220 West Lomita Avenue
Ojal, CA 93023
oakgroveschool.org

**INDIA**

**Rishi Valley Education Centre**
Rishi Valley Post
Chittoor District, 517 352, A.P.
www.rishivalley.org

**Rajghat Education Centre**
Rajghat
Fort Varanasi 221001, U.P.
www.rajghatbesantschool.org

**The Valley School**
Thatguni Post
Kanakapura Road
Bangalore 560 082
www.thevalleyschool.info

**The School KFI**
S.No. 82/3A2 & 82/5A2B
Solai Street, Thazhambur
Chennai–600 130
www.theschoolkfi.org

**Sahyadri School**
Post Tiwai Hill, Taluk Rajgurunagar Dist.
Pune 410 513, India
www.sahyadrischool.org

**Pathashaala KFI**
Elumichampattu
Tamil Nadu 603405
pcfl-kfi.org/pathashaala

— *Krishnamurti Foundations* —

**UK**

**Krishnamurti Foundation Trust, Ltd.**
Brockwood Park
Bramdean, Hampshire SO24 OLQ
www.kfoundation.org

**USA**

**Krishnamurti Foundation of America**
P.O. Box 1560

Ojai CA 93024
www.kfa.org

## INDIA

**Krishnamurti Foundation India**
Vasanta Vihar 64-65
Greenways Road Chennai, 600 028
www.kfionline.org

## LATIN AMERICA

**Fundacion Krishnamurti Latino Americana**
Spain
www.fkla.org

# INDEX

# KRISHNAMURTI FOUNDATION OF AMERICA

The Krishnamurti Foundation of America was founded in 1969 in Ojai, California, USA. The purpose of the Krishnamurti Foundation of America (KFA) is to preserve and disseminate the teachings of J. Krishnamurti and advance public understanding and realization of human potential by means of the study of these teachings. Their activities are focused on making the teachings available through traditional and modern media, outreach programs both in the USA and internationally, and through an adult Educational Center and School in Ojai.

Our challenge is to make Krishnamurti's teachings available to all age groups, different cultures, economic groups and races, and to do this we continue to expand our dissemination efforts.